# Mallory Didn't Want Jackson Knowing That Joshua Was His Son.

All her little fantasies notwithstanding, she'd already made up her mind that she wasn't going to tell Jackson that he was the father. Above all else, she didn't want Jackson feeling obligated to provide for her. She didn't want anything from him that he felt he *had* to give.

What she wanted from Jackson was his heart, something he wasn't about to offer. And there was no way he would ever marry her. He valued his freedom too much.

Besides, it would only confuse Joshua to have his father whimsically moving in and out of his life, disrupting it each time he turned up.

Just the way he'd disrupted *her* life now, by returning to her....

Dear Reader,

Welcome to the wonderful world of Silhouette Desire! This month, look for six scintillating love stories. I know you're going to enjoy them all. First up is *The Beauty, the Beast and the Baby*, a fabulous MAN OF THE MONTH from Dixie Browning. It's also the second book in her TALL, DARK AND HANDSOME miniseries.

The exciting SONS AND LOVERS series also continues with Leanne Banks's *Ridge: The Avenger*. This is Leanne's first Silhouette Desire, but she certainly isn't new to writing romance.

This month, Desire has *Husband: Optional*, the next installment of Marie Ferrarella's THE BABY OF THE MONTH CLUB. Don't worry if you've missed earlier titles in this series, because this book "stands alone." And it's so charming and breezy you're sure to just love it!

The WEDDING BELLES series by Carole Buck is completed with *Zoe and the Best Man*. This series just keeps getting better and better, and Gabriel Flynn is one scrumptious hero.

Next is Kristin James' Desire, *The Last Groom on Earth*, a delicious opposites-attract story written with Kristin's trademark sensuality.

Rounding out the month is an amnesia story (one of my *favorite* story twists), *Just a Memory Away*, by award-winning author Helen R. Myers.

And *next* month, we're beginning CELEBRATION 1000, a very exciting, ultraspecial three-month promotion celebrating the publication of the 1000th Silhouette Desire. During April, May and June, look for books by some of your most beloved writers, including Mary Lynn Baxter, Annette Broadrick, Joan Johnston, Cait London, Ann Major and Diana Palmer, who is actually writing book #1000! These will be months to remember, filled with "keepers."

As always, I wish you the very best,

Lucia Macro
Senior Editor

---

Please address questions and book requests to:
Silhouette Reader Service
U.S.: 3010 Walden Ave., P.O. Box 1325, Buffalo, NY 14269
Canadian: P.O. Box 609, Fort Erie, Ont. L2A 5X3

# MARIE FERRARELLA

## Husband: Optional

SILHOUETTE *Desire*®

Published by Silhouette Books

America's Publisher of Contemporary Romance

To
Isabel Swift, Leslie Wainger
&
Lucia Macro,
with thanks for letting me come home again.
I had a ball.

 SILHOUETTE BOOKS

ISBN 0-373-05988-4

HUSBAND: OPTIONAL

Copyright © 1996 by Marie Rydzynski-Ferrarella

**Printed in U.S.A.**

**Books by Marie Ferrarella**

Silhouette Desire
*Husband: Optional #988

Silhouette Romance
The Gift #588
Five-Alarm Affair #613
Heart to Heart #632
Mother for Hire #686
Borrowed Baby #730
Her Special Angel #744
The Undoing of Justin
   Starbuck #766
Man Trouble #815
The Taming of the Teen #839
Father Goose #869
Babies on His Mind #920
The Right Man #932
In Her Own Backyard #947
Her Man Friday #959
Aunt Connie's Wedding #984
†Caution: Baby Ahead #1007
†Mother on the Wing #1026
†Baby Times Two #1037
Father in the Making #1078
The Women in
   Joe Sullivan's Life #1096

Silhouette Books
Silhouette Christmas Stories 1992
"The Night Santa Claus Returned"

Silhouette Special Edition
It Happened One Night #597
A Girl's Best Friend #652
Blessing in Disguise #675
Someone To Talk To #703
World's Greatest Dad #767
Family Matters #832
She Got Her Man #843
Baby in the Middle #892
Husband: Some Assembly
   Required #931
Brooding Angel #963
*Baby's First Christmas #997

Silhouette Intimate Moments
‡Holding Out for a Hero #496
‡Heroes Great and Small #501
‡Christmas Every Day #538
Callaghan's Way #601
Caitlin's Guardian Angel #661
*Happy New Year—Baby! #686

Silhouette Yours Truly
*The 7lb., 2oz. Valentine

†Baby's Choice
‡Those Sinclairs
*The Baby of the Month Club

**Books by Marie Ferrarella writing as Marie Nicole**

Silhouette Desire
Tried and True #112
Buyer Beware #142
Through Laughter and Tears #161
Grand Theft: Heart #182
A Woman of Integrity #197
Country Blue #224
Last Year's Hunk #274
Foxy Lady #315
Chocolate Dreams #346
No Laughing Matter #382

Silhouette Romance
Man Undercover #373
Please Stand By #394
Mine by Write #411
Getting Physical #440

## MARIE FERRARELLA

lives in Southern California. She describes herself as the tired
mother of two overenergetic children and the contented wife of
one wonderful man. She is thrilled to be following her dream of
writing full-time.

Mallory Flannigan

is proud to

announce the

early arrival of

her son, Joshua,

who blew in

like a lion cub

# One

"Is it mine?"

The low voice was a mixture of stunned surprise, anger and a third, completely different emotion that Mallory couldn't begin to identify. It rumbled through the small, modern wood and glass real estate office like the first distant echo of thunder on a cloudy spring morning.

Or the wind blowing in like a lion at the first inkling of March. But this lion would never become a lamb.

Caught utterly unprepared, her head turned away from the speaker, Mallory Flannigan dropped the paperwork on the Melville house she had just spent the last half hour organizing. Two dozen sheets slid from her limp fingers, landing haphazardly on an oatmeal-colored industrial carpet.

Stunned, she was vaguely aware of stepping on several pages as she swung around to look at the man who had growled the question at her. Though there wasn't a chance in hell that she was wrong, Mallory fervently prayed that by some miracle, the voice didn't belong to Jackson Cain.

The prayer dissolved almost as quickly as her knees did.

Grasping a corner of the nearest desk for support, Mallory found herself looking up into Jackson's light green eyes. Light green eyes filled with complete disbelief as they washed over her.

He looked exactly the way she would have prophesied he would when he made the discovery that she was pregnant. Exactly the way she didn't want him to look. And it was for that reason, along with a trunk full of pride she had no idea what to do with, that she instinctively and immediately lied to him.

"No, it's not." Mallory looked away, dismissing his presence just the way he had once dismissed hers. "And, oh yes, hello to you after all these months."

Forcing herself to ignore her racing pulse, her suddenly aching, constricted heart and the overwhelming headache that had just materialized, full-blown, out of nowhere, Mallory faced a far more tenuous and challenging task: getting down on the floor to pick up the papers she had just dropped.

Still not looking at him, she gingerly lowered herself to the rug and began gathering the scattered sheets together.

*Why did he have to look like that when he asked? Damn him, anyway!*

*What did you expect? Hearts and flowers? You know what he's like.*

Mallory's angry retort, framed in cold indignation, rang in Jackson's ears. It wasn't his. No matter how angry she was, Mallory would never lie to him. He knew that for a fact.

Not exactly the way he had pictured their reunion, but he was relieved at her disclaimer about the baby.

Wasn't he?

Of course he was. A man didn't want to travel clear across the country to see a woman he had been fantasizing about for the last seven months, a woman he had tried to siphon out of his blood like an encroaching, all-encompassing disease, just to discover that she was pregnant with his child. Right?

Breath backing up in his lungs, Jackson reminded himself that it was for this reason that he'd left the coast and Mallory in the first place, to get away from involvement. To stop what he saw was happening in his life. The blotting out of his own soul. Being with Mallory, sharing his life with her, was taking away pieces of himself, vital pieces he desperately needed in order to work.

A baby would have meant involvement to the nth degree and destroyed life as he knew it and foresaw it to be. He was glad it wasn't his.

So why was there this incredible sting of disappointment humming through his entire being? And betrayal. He felt a sense of betrayal that was so large it almost swallowed him up whole.

Betrayal almost as huge as the baby that rounded out her stomach. A once flat stomach, Jackson remembered involuntarily, that had quivered beneath the slightest touch of his fingertips.

He shook his head, not in answer to any question, spoken or otherwise, but just to clear it, like a dog trying to rid itself of unwanted moisture clinging to its body.

Jackson came to an instant later and realized that Mallory was on the floor, picking up the papers she had dropped when she saw him. Joining her, he quickly reached for the scattered sheets, shoving them together into a pile. His eyes never left her.

She was pregnant. Pregnant. He was no expert, but she was so large, she had to be at least seven months along, if not more. He'd only been gone for seven months. Had she taken a lover immediately?

The question burned in his brain.

"Here," he growled, unable to manage the anger he felt yet, "you shouldn't be on the floor doing that in your condition."

For a second, Mallory didn't trust her voice enough to make a reply. Her throat was brimming with so many diverse emotions.

Damn, she'd dreamt about him. Night after night, Jackson had come to her, unbidden, in her sleep. Returned to her to tell her that he'd been wrong to ever leave. That he loved her and wanted her.

Wanted to share his life with her.

In each dream, each fantasy, there'd been love in his eyes, the same kind of love that there had been that wondrous night when they had unwittingly created this child whose heart beat beneath hers. Love, not anger.

The anger that was in Jackson's eyes now.

*If looks could kill...* she thought. Well, they couldn't. And what did he have to be upset about anyway? Any anger rightfully belonged to her.

"What should I be doing in my condition?" Irritation snapped and crackled in her voice. "I'm afraid that I'm not like you, Jackson. There's no bank account waiting for me to tap into. No family inheritance to lean on." Or family, for that matter, she added silently. There'd been no one for her to turn to when the stick had turned pink, even if her independent nature had allowed her to lean on someone. "I can't just pick up and go like the wind whenever I want to. I have a living to earn." Without meaning to, she glanced down at her stomach. "And bills to pay."

It wasn't the bills she resented, Mallory thought, silently apologizing to her unborn baby. She was comfortable enough. And even if she wasn't, she would have found a way to pay the costs. She wanted this baby, wanted to hold the only real symbol of the love she had once foolishly thought, dreamed, hoped, was so perfect. Wanted this baby more than anything else in the world because it undoubtedly represented what was the best part of both of them.

Certainly it was the best thing that Jackson had ever done, the rat.

It was Jackson she resented. Jackson, with his cavalier way of dropping out and now into her life when the whim carried him. Jackson, who should have cared enough to remain in the first place.

Mallory tried not to glare as she took the papers from his hand with a jerk, but it wasn't easy. It was difficult not to glare at the man who made her feel loved, then disappeared, leaving her behind without any attempt at further communication for seven months. Not a note, not a phone call. Nothing. Not once had he tried to get in contact with her to find out how she was getting along without him.

Not that she would have told him. But it would have given her some measure of satisfaction to slam the telephone in his ear, or send back a ripped up letter.

Jackson rose to his feet. Mallory remained where she was, on her knees with papers clutched in her hands. Silently, he offered his hand to her and waited.

She didn't take it immediately. If there'd been any other way to get up, she would have. She wanted nothing to do with him. That included his hand.

But her pregnancy had been difficult for her from the very beginning. It was a struggle she had managed to work around, but being eight and a half months pregnant was a contest in endurance that went beyond fighting her way into panty hose.

With a sigh, she realized that there was no way she was getting off this floor without help. She was the only one here right now. Everyone else who worked in the office was either out to lunch, showing a house or beating the bushes for new houses to list.

Mallory was stuck. It was either take Jackson's hand or remain where she was. Her back began aching again. Damn, where were the people who were always hanging around here when you needed them?

She glanced toward the door, hoping someone would come in. The door remained closed.

Biting her lower lip, she raised her hand to Jackson's and grudgingly wrapped her fingers around the long artistic hand she'd once admired so. Hands that could make her body sing.

For a split second, Jackson didn't know if Mallory was actually taking the help he silently offered, or if she was trying to wrestle him to the ground. He had to brace his legs to keep from falling into her. His fingers fairly throbbed as Mallory pulled herself up.

She certainly didn't look that big, or that strong, Jackson thought, shoving his hand into the back pocket of his jeans.

"Thank you," Mallory said icily, turning away from him.

Jackson stared at the back of her head, thinking. Pride nettled him. He followed Mallory to her desk in the corner of the office.

"If it's not mine, whose is it?"

Mallory had always been stubborn, as stubborn as hell. Maybe, he acknowledged unwillingly, even as stubborn as he was. It would be just like her not to tell him. But he needed to know.

His eyes swept over her form again. This *had* to be his child. The timing was right. He'd left her seven months ago.

Seven months, one week and two days. Long enough for any woman to seep out of a man's mind, not linger there like traces of summer smoke. Or like the scent of fresh spring flowers, refusing to leave, to dissipate.

After all this time, why was she still there, haunting him? Making him want her?

And why was she lying to him now?

He hoped to God she was lying to him now.

But even as he asked, he knew that she wasn't. Mallory could no more lie about something like that than he could set up housekeeping and become domesticated.

His eyes looked like green embers, burning straight into her, Mallory thought. Only sheer stubbornness prevented her from backing away. She'd loved his intense eyes once.

His intense manner. Hell, she had loved everything about him, even his faults.

But she'd been young and stupid all those months ago. A baby was not the only thing that had grown within her. Her maturity and integrity had grown as well, enabling her to answer the question he asked calmly, intelligently.

"What, you think you're the only man to walk the face of the earth?" she heard herself shouting at him. "I assure you, Jackson Cain, there's at least one other of your species who I found just as exciting, just as wonderful, just as pleasurable as you." She paused, gathering strength. "More."

Each word she uttered slashed at him. His eyes darkened. "Who?"

He looked like a dark, brooding prince, moving restlessly along the castle's rampart. Well, he could just damn well fall off the ramparts for all she cared.

Her voice rose higher. "What gives you the right to come stomping back into my life after all this time and demand to know intimate details? You gave all that up, remember?"

He wasn't here to debate delicacies or semantics. He wanted an answer.

"Who?" Jackson demanded again. He leaned over the desk, his voice lower, his anger higher. "Who's the baby's father, Mallory?"

Mallory cupped her hand protectively around the baby's shape. She hadn't contemplated having to lie to Jackson. That wasn't the way her fantasy about his return into her life had gone.

A sharp pain intruded into her thoughts and she banished it, trying to think.

Her mind felt like a slate hastily wiped clean of everything. She realized that she was staring past Jackson's head at the framed collage on the back wall. A collage of all the real estate agents who comprised Gateway Estates.

Names beneath the miniature photographs jumped up at her. Desperate, angry, Mallory combined two of them at random.

"Steven. Steven Mitchell." She raised her chin pugnaciously. She might be huge with child, but her spirit hadn't abated one iota. That was the first thing they had discovered they had in common. Pride, in huge doses. "And what damn business is it of yours who my baby's father is?"

He wanted to take Mallory by the shoulders and shake her. Instead, he shoved his hands deeper into his pockets, fitting them in the small, tight space.

"Because I think you're lying." He said it with a conviction he didn't feel.

Angry tears threatened to completely overwhelm her. Only sheer will kept them under restraint. Mallory stuck her chin out farther, giving him an excellent target and daring him to make use of it. She slapped the papers down on the desk in front of her, her eyes like glowing lasers of indignation.

"Lying?" Eyes wide with shock, Mallory spat the word at him. "You think I'm *lying?*"

All the anger that had been stored up within her over the last seven months now fueled the fire she felt in her veins. A tiger on the scent of prey, Mallory rounded her desk and went in for the attack. She jabbed her index finger in the middle of his chest. A chest she had once adored leaning her head against.

"I'm not the one given to making things up, Jackson. You are."

He had no idea what she was talking about. When had he lied to her? Jackson quickly examined his memory and came up empty. He'd never lied to her. Except for once, he'd been very careful with his words. They were his medium.

Jackson stared at fury encapsulated in the form of a five foot seven inch woman who glowed with indignation and motherhood.

"I'm a writer, Mallory." He grabbed the finger she was burrowing into his chest and firmly moved it to the side. "It's my job to make things up."

Was it his job to lie to her as well? Her eyes blazed even as another pointy shaft of pain drove through her. She ignored it. It paled beside her ire. Did he think she was some sort of idiot, to toy with and then discard? "To everyone?"

What did she mean by that? "Anyone who buys my book—" This time, he did grab her shoulders. But he didn't shake her. It wasn't easy, but he didn't. He just held her in place. "Look, just what are—?"

Mallory yanked free of his hold, taking a half step back. "Well, I bought your book. And I bought you—and every damn word you said."

She was admitting too much. Her mind flashed Mayday but the hurt she felt made the message difficult to assimilate in time.

Mallory cleared her throat. She stopped, trying to reclaim her dignity. Her voice dropped an octave. "Or at least, *I* did." Her eyes hardened as she turned them on him again. "But that's not the point."

Dignity recovered, Mallory wrapped it around her shoulders, a precious shawl to make her impervious to anything else Jackson Cain might say. And just maybe, to the look in his eyes which threatened to undo her completely.

With determination, she moved away from him.

There was no way in the world that she was going to give him the satisfaction of telling him that this was his baby. Not after he'd walked out on her, leaving nothing but a lame excuse hanging in the air. Leaving her to be alone again.

Well, she wasn't alone anymore. She had this baby and when it was born, they were going to form a family unit. The baby was going to be her family. Her world. She didn't need a man who couldn't keep his word, even if it had been tendered through deeds and feelings rather than actual syllables.

And if it hurt him to think that she had easily replaced him with another man after he left, well, that was just icing on the cake.

Part of him wanted to leave, to have done with all this. But the rest of Jackson wasn't listening. The rest of him had to know.

"What *is* the point?" he demanded, following her to the file cabinet.

She shoved the drawer she had just opened shut again. The sound reverberated through the office. Damn, why hadn't someone returned yet? He couldn't shout at her like this if someone else was in the office. Could he?

"The point is," she informed him tersely, "I moved on with my life."

"Obviously."

His eyes skimmed over her rounded shape. Her belly was ripely evident despite the roomy two-piece green outfit she was wearing. Damn, why didn't he just go?

Because he couldn't.

He'd gone to New York to get away, to clear his mind and his life of her. It hadn't helped.

Mallory had invaded his space every day while he was away, despite the distance there was between them. The distance and the silence he had so deliberately enforced, all to no avail.

In the end, Jackson found that he couldn't weed her out of his thoughts any more than a man could do battle with the wind. Every time he thought that he had finally succeeded in shutting his mind to her, another memory would crop up. Another moment they had shared would return to haunt him.

Anything could trigger it. No matter how hard he tried, there was always something else that would remind him of her. She was like a fever of the blood and he had no cure.

They'd had four months together. Four very heated, intense months that had threatened to shut him off from everything but her. He was afraid that he was becoming consumed with Mallory and that his consumption would destroy his creativity. So he had left. Ran, actually, to preserve himself and life as he knew it.

It hadn't worked. He had brought her with him, in his mind.

He'd returned to see Mallory just one more time, to convince himself that she was only a flesh-and-blood woman, not a myth, not a goddess, not a dream he had conjured up and certainly not something that had managed to become larger than his own existence.

He'd returned to see her and then move on with his life.

So now he saw. Saw what a fool he'd been. While he had lain awake in his own bed, thinking of her, unable to find solace in anyone else's arms although he had tried—and failed before he'd ever taken even one of the women who threw themselves at him to bed—all that time, Mallory had been with another man. Made love with another man and created a child.

While he had longed for her, she had been with this Steven Mitchell. He hated the very sound of the man's name.

Jackson could taste his own fury, his own bile in his mouth. The passion that went into making him a bestselling mystery author, the depth of passion that he had physically shared only with Mallory, threatened to erupt now in the face of this betrayal.

If she had sense, she'd be afraid. But anger, hurt and this damn pain that was traveling through her on pointy stilts had muted her feelings of self-preservation. Instead, his anger goaded her on.

"Don't you look at me like that, Jackson Cain," she warned.

Did she have any idea how much he wanted to strangle her? "Like what?"

If she had the strength, she would have beat on him with fisted hands. As it was, it was all Mallory could do just to remain standing. She suddenly felt weak. But her anger managed to sustain her.

"Like this is a biblical movie and you're looking around for a rock to toss at me." She saw the denial forming on his lips but she wouldn't let it emerge. She wasn't through with him yet.

*You'll never be through with him,* a small voice echoed within her. She did her best to ignore it.

"You left me, remember?" she demanded. If Jackson wanted to answer her, she wasn't ready to hear his excuses. "Left me because you had to get on with your work and I was in the way."

Did he have any idea how much that had hurt her? To have him think that she wanted to do anything that would jeopardize who and what he was? She had accepted him, wanted him, just the way he was, not to conform to some image she had created.

And he had still left.

"What was I supposed to do, sit home alone at night and do readings in your honor?" Except for the last part, it was exactly what she had done. Stayed home alone and cursed his memory.

She'd even ripped apart a few of his books, but it hadn't made her feel any better. Nothing had, until she had discovered that she was pregnant. She'd taken refuge in that, in planning a future for herself and her unborn baby.

Jackson frowned. She made him sound like some sort of a pompous fool. And he wasn't. At least not pompous. He wasn't quite so sure about the fool part. If anything, he'd been a fool with a capital *F.* A fool to have dreamed about her so much. To have wanted her so that every fiber of his body ached from sheer memory.

"If you had, it doesn't look as if you read for very long." His eyes damned the shape she had taken on. How could she have done that? How could she? "How long did it take, Mallory? How long did it take you to get over me? A day? A week? An hour?"

Her chin went up again. He had no right to act like the spurned lover, not when he was the one who had done the spurning.

"Science hasn't invented a measurement that small yet, but they're working on it." Her eyes narrowed as she looked at his chest. "I suggested using your heart as a guideline."

His eyes narrowed into slits. "I would have thought you would have volunteered yours under the circumstances. Or couldn't they find that, either? Was it missing, along with your loyalty?"

Damn, it wasn't supposed to hurt like this, thinking of her being with another man. But it did. It hurt like hell. Like someone had just set his gut on fire and walked away, laughing.

"Loyalty?" Her voice was hollow as it echoed the word. Mallory almost choked on it as she stared at him incredulously. "Loyalty? To what? A man who holds you in his arms, tells you that you mean so much to him and then leaves?"

Jackson remembered exactly what she was referring to. That had happened in a moment of weakness, nothing more, he'd told himself over and over again. He hadn't meant to say those words. Or at least, he hadn't meant to say them aloud.

But that didn't change anything. "How long did you wait, Mallory?" he demanded again. Had there been someone else all along? While he had held her and loved her, had there been someone else she had turned to when he wasn't there? He had to know. "How long?"

Mallory opened her mouth to shout another lie at him, but the pain sucked the words away from her lips. The pain, hot and overwhelming this time, took over every limb of her body and wrenched them until all her attention was focused on it. Her eyes flew open wide with stunned amazement and disbelief. Everything else faded.

A strangled gasp escaped her lips.

The argument disappeared as if it had never existed. Jackson grabbed Mallory just as she swayed. Turning pale, she looked as if she were going to crumple right in front of him.

"Mallory, what's the matter?" He tightened his arms around her shoulders, holding her upright.

She wanted to shrug him off, wanted to walk away on her own power. But she couldn't move, couldn't do anything. Pain had galvanized her to the rug.

"I don't know— I..."

For a moment, there was no breath available for her to say anything. She couldn't push any of the words out past the wall of pain encompassing her.

Jackson looked around for someone, anyone, to help them. But the small office was just as deserted as it had been when he had first entered it. He vaguely remembered that it had always seemed so crowded to him whenever he'd come by to take Mallory to lunch. Why wasn't anyone here now?

Still holding her firmly by the shoulders, Jackson began to ease Mallory into a chair. "Maybe you'd better sit down."

"Very astute." Mallory gritted the words out between her teeth. She felt her bottom make contact. "I always loved the quickness of your mind."

The room was suddenly beginning to grow dim. Mallory struggled to focus on something, anything, to bring it back. The frightening thought that she was going to faint wafted through her.

No, she wasn't, she wasn't going to swoon like some idiotic heroine in a grade B melodrama. That was all she had to do, faint with Jackson here.

Her breathing was becoming labored, Jackson realized. He wasn't a man to panic, but then, he'd never held a fainting pregnant woman in his arms, either. Maybe he should call 911.

Jackson began to ease his hand away from her shoulders, trying to reach for the telephone on her desk. Mallory clutched at his wrist, stopping him.

"Jackson." His name was a breathless whisper on her lips.

Concerned, he dropped to his knees beside her. "What?"

On his knees, that's the way she'd wanted him, she thought. On his knees, begging her to accept his apology. It didn't seem to matter now. "I think I know what's wrong now."

She was completely drenched in less than a minute. Jackson wiped the hair away from her forehead. It was falling into her eyes. "What?"

Mallory wet her lips. The other end of her was suddenly wet as well. It was all the confirmation she needed.

"I'm having the baby."

# Two

---

Mallory's words rang in his ears. Jackson stared at her. She couldn't actually be serious, could she? "You're what?"

If this was what labor felt like, this baby was going to be an only child, Mallory swore to herself. There was no way she was going to go through this more than once.

"Are you deaf as well as heartless?" Mallory gasped. Pain and fear mingled and swirled within a black cauldron through her body and soul. "I'm having the baby."

He attempted to pry her hand from his wrist, amazed at the effort it required. She was holding on to him like a survivor of a shipwreck held on to a floating board. For the time being, he let her hand remain.

"Now?"

Had the months in New York made him stupid? "No, a year from now. Yes, now," she snapped at Jackson. With her free hand, she held on to her stomach as if that could somehow keep the baby housed where it was a little longer. *"Now,"* she screamed as another contraction ripped through her with the power and breadth of an all-consuming hurricane.

Jackson's eyes were drawn to her heaving abdomen. He half expected to see a baby emerge, propelled out by the force of her scream that was now ricocheting throughout the wood and glass office. Pulling his hand free, Jackson reached for the telephone again. Déjà vu struck as Mallory grasped his hand, yanking it to her even harder than the first time.

What was he doing? This was no time for telephone calls. She had to get to the hospital as soon as possible. "Take me."

Take her. That was all he had thought about these last few months. Taking her. Taking her on the kitchen table, the coffee table, the living room floor. The beach at twilight. Everywhere and anywhere. In absence, Mallory possessed his mind more firmly than she had when they had been together.

But this was certainly not the time to live out any of his fantasies, even if this Steven character hadn't entered into the picture.

With patience he didn't know he was capable of, Jackson smiled at her. Gentleness and all the tender feelings that were there just a breath beneath the surface rose up.

"Mallory, I'd love to take you, but I think you need a doctor more than me right now."

It took a moment for his words to register through the haze of pain. When had he become such an egotist? Had that happened after he left her? He hadn't been one during the time they spent together. But then, maybe she hadn't really known him at all.

"No," she nearly shouted. "Take me to... the hospital. Drive."

Oh God, they were coming hard and fast now, she thought, her panic mounting. The contractions were bursting over her like cannon fire, devastating and without warning.

To the hospital. Of course that's what she meant by "Take me." It was only his own desires getting in the way, making him misinterpret her words. They were the ones he had secretly hoped he'd hear when he saw her again and at the time they'd had nothing to do with babies and rides to the hospital.

All water under the wrong bridge now, he thought looking at her.

"That's what I'm trying to do," he told her. One hand still very much trapped in hers, he pulled the telephone toward him on the desk with his other. "I'm calling for an ambulance."

She shook her head from side to side. The mere motion made her dizzy. Mallory gulped in air, desperately trying to find a way to make the contractions abate long enough for her to think coherently.

Damn, the pain was all around her. There was nowhere to go, no escape.

"No time. Hospital's right here." Jackson was looking at her blankly, as if she were speaking in a foreign tongue. Didn't he understand anything? "Harris Memorial. Here."

The last word emerged as a piercing screech. If she didn't know any better, she would have said her baby was trying to kick its way out of her womb, like a martial arts expert.

Belatedly, Jackson realized what she was trying to say. The hospital she was referring to was only three miles up the road. It would probably take the ambulance more time to arrive here and then take her than it would for him to drive over to the hospital in the first place.

"Okay, we'll drive. I'll drive," he corrected.

Panic was a very odd sensation for Jackson. He couldn't recall ever having experienced it before, not in any manner, shape or form. But it was clearly nibbling away at his nerves now. He had to get her to the hospital. Fast.

He'd come here on his Harley. The bike, his very first love, had been his means of transportation to and from New York as well, much to the heartfelt distress of his anxious publisher. But while it suited all of his needs, Jackson knew he couldn't very well take her to the hospital like that.

"All right, all right," Jackson said soothingly, trying to calm himself as well as her. This wasn't going down as his finest hour, he thought. "We'll have to take your car." He looked around the office as if seeing it for the first time. "Where are your keys?"

The gut-wrenching wave of pain passed. Mallory managed to muster what would have passed for a grimace under other circumstances. She was trying for a semblance of a smile.

"You rode your motorcycle here, right?"

"Right."

He began opening the drawers on her desk, starting with the bottom one. Deeper than the ones above it, it was loaded down with catalogues for baby clothes, toys and furniture. Frustrated, Jackson slammed it shut and opened the one on the other side.

"I don't think it'll do much for your dignity or the baby's health, to ride to the hospital on top of the Harley." Not to mention that he wasn't all that sure both of them could fit on it, not in her present condition. But he thought it best not to mention that. A woman's vanity went deep and this wasn't the time to rankle it. "You might jar it loose."

"That might not be so ba-add."

When he looked up at her, he saw that her eyes had grown huge again, signaling another onslaught of pain. The deep, guttural moan from her lips confirmed it.

Jackson pulled open a third drawer and struck pay dirt. "Got it."

He held up her purse like a trophy. The weight registered a moment later. Her shoulder bag felt as if it weighed a ton. How did she manage to walk with this much added weight hanging from her shoulder, especially at a time like this? She had more in her purse than he had packed up when he left for New York. Everything he'd owned went into storage.

Including, he'd thought, his heart.

His eyes slanted toward Mallory and he knew he had thought wrong. Even belonging to another man and pregnant with his child, Mallory was still the most desirable woman he had ever set eyes on.

A woman he still wanted.

There was no time to think about that. No time for anything but getting her to the hospital as soon as humanly possible. Rummaging through the debris in her purse, Jackson found her key ring just as she gasped again. The purse dropped from his hands as he pulled out the ring. He grabbed her, afraid that she was going to pass out.

"I'm okay. For now," she managed.

Releasing her, he looked down at the metal ring in his hand. It held an entire array of keys on it.

"Which one, Mallory?" He jingled it to catch her attention when she didn't look his way.

There had to be a dozen keys on the ring, if not more. If he tried each one, they'd be here until the baby was celebrating its first birthday.

Mallory blinked, trying to focus on the ring Jackson dangled in front of her. They all looked alike to her, keys to the various lock boxes that were on the different houses which were listed under her name at the agency.

Her teeth sank into her lower lip as she pointed to one. Another contraction was coming.

"That. That one," she added for emphasis. "Hurry, Jackson, please hurry."

She knew it sounded as if she were begging, and maybe she was. Begging for this to be over. Begging to be taken to someone who could help her somehow get away from this pain.

Jackson yanked the car key free of the ring, afraid that if he dropped the keys, he wouldn't be able to zero in on the right one in time. Right about now, he sincerely wished he had hurried. Hurried back to her seven months ago instead of now. Either that, or had managed to extricate her from his mind instead of returning to find her like this, rounded out with another man's love.

Bracing his hands on her shoulders to hold her steady, he asked, "Can you get up?"

Her legs felt like useless appendages. Mallory shook her head. "I don't..."

Jackson didn't wait for her to finish. Instead, he picked Mallory up in his arms. Behind him, he heard the door opening.

He turned around with Mallory in his arms in time to see a tall, slender blonde entering the real estate office. As soon as she saw them, the woman ran in, concern etched on her face, her eyes on Mallory.

She looked from Mallory to the man holding her. Marlene Travis knew she didn't recognize him. But that wasn't important right now. Only Mallory was. "Mallory, are you all right?"

"No, she's not all right, she's having a baby," Jackson retorted, trying to edge his way past the woman.

Hurrying to the door, Marlene swung it wide open for them. She'd gone through the same experience nearly three months ago herself. Except that her baby had been delivered in an elevator during the season's worst storm. It was a story to tell Robby as soon as he was old enough to understand. A story he'd probably take glee in repeating.

Marlene followed them out to the parking lot. "How far apart?" she asked Mallory. "The contractions, how far apart are they?"

Mallory huddled in the shelter of Jackson's arms, if a hugely pregnant woman could huddle, she thought sarcastically.

"They're not," Mallory cried out. And here came another one.

Jackson felt Mallory bracing herself and stiffening in his arms. "Oh God," he groaned under his breath.

First babies were supposed to take their time, Marlene thought, but hers hadn't. She hoped that Mallory made it to the hospital in time.

"It'll be all right," she promised with a note of conviction she could only hope fooled Mallory. "I'll call the hospital to let them know you're coming. And Dr. Pollack," she added quickly. "I'll call her, too. Go, go," Marlene urged Jackson as she turned to run back into the office.

Go? What did she think he was doing, playing tag? Hell, for that matter, what did *he* think he was doing here? Where the hell was Steven when she needed him? He should be the one here, not him.

The question hovered on his lips. He tabled it. Now wasn't the best time to ask.

Still holding her, Jackson tested the handle on her car. It gave easily. Pulling the door open, he set Mallory into the passenger seat as gently as he could, all things considered.

The strangest things flittered through his mind as he rounded the hood and got in on the driver's side. "Still leaving your doors unlocked?" He put the key into the ignition.

"Yes." She was forgetful. Was he going to reprimand her about that now? "Drive," Mallory ordered, squirming in her seat. The seat belt wouldn't fit around her. "Blood's hard to get out of upholstery."

And wasn't that a cheerful picture? Jackson slid the metal tongue into the slot for her, securing the seat belt. Turning the key, he stepped on the accelerator. "Yes, ma'am."

Mallory would have hit him if she had the strength.

Jackson was accustomed to weaving his Harley in and out of tight places. Mallory's car was less accommodating, but he managed just the same. He made it to the hospital in five minutes flat, going through yellow lights and pushing his luck as he sped through the moderate traffic that flowed over the Newport Beach roads.

As he looked to the left he saw the tall tower, the symbol of Harris Memorial, looming just ahead. Goal's end, he thought.

He glanced at Mallory. Hands wrapped around her purse, her knuckles were turning white. Almost as white as her face. Compassion mingled with pity. Jealousy had no place here between them, not now. "Want me to call Steven for you?"

Jackson's voice played in her head. Mallory blinked as she turned to look at him. "Who?"

"Steven, your lover," he added when she still didn't respond. The very word tasted briny on his tongue. It made him long for a tall, cold beer to wash the bad flavor out of his mouth.

Steven. Right, the man she'd made up. She'd almost forgotten about that. The last fifteen minutes had felt like an eternity to her. "He's not here."

Jackson glanced at her as he took the corner, turning onto the road that fed into the hospital grounds. "Obviously."

*Think, Mallory, think.* But it was hard to string coherent thoughts together when she felt as if she were being torn apart.

"No, he's not here on the coast. I—" She didn't have time to make up any more lies, the pain was blocking out everything. She grasped his wrist just as he pulled up in front of the emergency room. "It's going to come. Oh, Jackson, it's coming."

He could feel her panic as if it were a physical thing. Jackson stopped on a dime and was out of the car before the emergency brake had completely engaged. The car was still rocking to and fro as he slammed the door and hurried around to her side.

"Not without someone else around to help it's not," he ordered sternly. They'd made it, he thought. From here on in, Mallory would have the care she needed. And he didn't have to feel so completely inept.

He heard the sound of the electronic doors opening behind him. The next moment, men in white livery were beside him, angling him out of the way. An orderly butted a gurney up against the side of the car.

Whoever the blonde at the real estate office was, she'd lived up to her promise about calling the hospital, Jackson thought with relief. "It's going to be okay, Mallory," he promised her.

Pain flourished within her like weeds growing after the spring rain. Yet even so, there was one sharp beacon that rose up above the rest. Fear. She was scared.

Gentle hands drew her out of the car and onto the gurney. Mallory looked around, trying to find the one face she needed to see.

"Jackson?"

He elbowed his way in between the two orderlies and an older nurse with skin the color of coffee. Something he could use right about now, he thought.

Jackson grasped Mallory's hand. It felt incredibly icy to him. "Right here, Mal."

She'd probably regret saying this later. But later didn't count. Only now did. "Stay with me."

Very carefully, the nurse broke the bond between Jackson and Mallory, extricating his hand. If he held on to her, it would only impede their progress.

"Your husband can come right up with you," she promised Mallory soothingly. Dark chocolate eyes turned to look at him, "C'mon,'Daddy,'" she instructed with a wide, infectious grin. "Time to see what your handiwork accomplished."

She winked broadly as she took him by the arm, then nodded at the orderly to take the gurney.

Jackson started to protest that it wasn't *his* handiwork that was about to make a debut, but the look on Mallory's face changed his mind. This jerk who had replaced him in her affections wasn't around and she needed someone. It looked as if he were elected.

"Okay." He walked quickly beside the gurney as the orderly pushed it toward the bank of elevators in the rear of the hospital.

Staring straight up, Mallory tried to focus her attention on the stream of light fixtures that whizzed by above her head and not her pain as they wheeled her down the hall and into the elevator. She tried to concentrate on Jackson's reappearance in her life. Desperate, she tried to think of anything besides the pain, anything at all. But it didn't work. The pain was all-consuming.

The lights on the elevator keyboard winked in and out as each floor passed. She wasn't going to make it, she thought. The baby was going to be born here, in an elevator, just like Marlene's had been.

"The baby is coming out," Mallory shrieked on the cusp of another contraction.

"Yes, honey, I know." Dark skin passed over light as the woman patted her hand.

"No, I have to push," Mallory cried. "Really." Didn't anyone understand?

Above her, the nurse exchanged glances with the orderly. Mallory couldn't see the expression on either face, but she could guess. They thought she was just being hysterical. But she wasn't. She knew her own body. The baby was coming.

"Dr. Pollack is already in the hospital. She was making her rounds when your friend called in," the nurse told her. "After she sees you, she'll decide whether or not—"

Mallory moved her head frantically back and forth, her dark hair fanned out against the sterile white sheet. "Decide nothing, it's coming now. I have to push."

They were the only ones in the service elevator. Still it was crammed. Jackson edged the nurse aside and took Mallory's hand in his, holding it tightly. Had it always felt this small, this helpless?

He fixed his eyes on hers. Jackson knew very little about what went on during this process when new life struggled into the world, but he had a feeling that Mallory couldn't just take matters into her own hands without a doctor present.

"Mallory, listen to me." He enunciated very slowly. "You have to wait for the doctor."

Typical man, he didn't understand anything. "You wait, I can't."

The elevator doors opened and the orderly immediately began to push the gurney out.

His fingers wrapped around hers for support, Jackson continued holding Mallory's hand as he moved quickly alongside the gurney.

"You have to wait." It was an order, not a request. Jackson didn't want anything happening to her. "She'll be with you in a couple of minutes."

"A couple of minutes'll be too late. I have to push now."

All the forces in the world were centered in her loins and they were urging her to bear down and push. She was at their mercy and felt completely helpless to do anything else but that.

Behind him, the nurse took control. "Breathe the way they taught you in class," she instructed.

Turning, the nurse nodded at the orderly, a silent command passing between them. He ran down the hall to the nurses' station, looking for Dr. Pollack. The nurse took the end of the gurney and maneuvered it into the labor room.

There were two beds in the room, both empty and pristine. Everything in the room was bright and fresh. Except for her, Mallory thought.

She clutched at Jackson's hand, squeezing hard. "But I have to push—"

"Breathe, damn it, Mallory, don't debate," Jackson ordered. Did she always have to be so stubborn about everything? They were only trying to help her. "Breathe. Now."

Her eyes fixed on his, a tiny spark reentering them, Mallory began to pant the way she'd learned to do in Lamaze class. A class she had attended by herself because there'd been no one she wanted to ask to accompany her. She'd taken the classes so that she could become prepared for what lay ahead. But nothing could have braced her for what she felt now.

It felt like two pairs of unseen hands were going to rip her apart at any second and she had no way to stop them.

Mallory was vaguely aware that someone was talking to her. Jackson? No, it was the nurse. The nurse was telling her something. As the pain receded, she stopped panting and listened.

"Okay, honey, we're going to have to transfer you onto the bed." Aligning the gurney with the closest bed, she positioned herself at one end, urging Jackson to stand on the opposite side. The orderly returned and she beckoned him over as well.

"I've got her!" the young man announced, indicating the woman following him.

Jackson turned to see a tall, regal-looking woman entering the room. Her blond hair was neatly arranged in a French twist that accentuated her striking cheekbones. She wore a long white coat which flowed around her as she hurried to the gurney.

But even the coarse lines of the coat didn't quite manage to hide the fact that she looked to be as pregnant as Mallory.

Jackson realized he was staring and quite probably had his mouth opened. He shut it again. "You're the doctor?"

Even though the room was brimming with agitation and turmoil, Sheila Pollack felt the man's eyes burrowing into her.

"Yes I am. Doctors are human too," she assured him with a patient smile.

Her own due date was still more than a month away and she intended to work up to the very end. She was strong and she enjoyed her work. Added to that, she had built up a very strong rapport with all of her patients, particularly the ones who were pregnant. It gave them all a common bond and empathy that no amount of money or textbook knowledge could ever provide.

Sheila turned toward Mallory. This one, she'd always known, was going to be a screamer. Her heart went out to the younger woman.

"Hi, Mallory. Ready?"

"Oh, so ready." Mallory ground out the words between clenched teeth.

"Okay, let's just see about that." Sheila nodded toward the nurse and orderly. "Why don't you hold off on the transfer until I check her out?"

The two stepped to the side as Sheila took a pair of thin rubber gloves from the dispenser on the wall and slipped them on with practiced grace. Her eyes never left Mallory's face.

"I spoke to Marlene personally." Her service had put the other woman through to her at the hospital immediately. "She made it sound as if you were ready to blow," she teased gently.

*And from the looks of it,* Sheila thought, *Marlene wasn't far from wrong.*

"Oh, I am, I am," Mallory gasped, forcing the words out in a pant. She was beginning to feel that she was never going to be able to utter a full sentence normally again.

It took only one look for Sheila to assess the situation. She dropped the sheet back into place and stripped off her gloves.

"Fully dilated and ready to go," she confirmed. "Nature is always the best judge in these matters." Sheila dropped the gloves into the wastebasket on the side of the bed. "Leave her on the gurney," she instructed the nurse. "And take her into the delivery room. We're about to have ourselves another little future tax payer." She stopped long enough to squeeze Mallory's hand reassuringly. "It's going to be over with before you know it. See you in five minutes," she promised.

Sheila began to leave the room and then looked questioningly at Jackson. He looked as if he were rooted to the spot. Early on in her pregnancy, as she sat shivering on the examining table in only a dressing gown, Mallory had broken down and told Sheila the whole story. Sobbing, trying to regain her dignity which seemed so very precious to her, Mallory had shown her the photograph of Jackson that she carried in her wallet.

He looked better in person, Sheila decided. A lot better. She was glad that Jackson had returned in time to see his baby born. She knew her patient well enough to know that Mallory would feel a great deal better having him in the delivery room with her.

"If you follow me, I can show you where to change," Sheila told Jackson.

"Change?" he echoed dumbly. Jackson stepped back as the nurse and orderly pushed Mallory's gurney out into the hall again.

"For the delivery," Sheila explained easily. "We like to keep things as sterile as possible. We're funny that way."

When he still seemed reluctant to move, Sheila hooked her arm through Jackson's and coaxed him gently out of the room.

The locker room where all the expectant fathers changed into hospital green was just down the hall, right next to the delivery room. The doctors' lockers were buffered on the other side.

He didn't know about this. It was one thing to stand beside Mallory in the labor room, offering moral support in lieu of the man who should have been there. But it was entirely another matter to take his place in the delivery room.

A place, a small voice reminded him, that could have been his had he remained where he should have remained.

"But I—"

"Returned just in time, didn't you?" She guided him down to the locker. Sheila sensed reluctance. Reluctance that only needed a little urging to disappear. She wasn't above pushing if the situation called for it. "It's right this way."

Jackson couldn't help feeling a little like a royalist being led to the guillotine.

# Three

___

God knows he'd written about it. More than once, actually. And, in writing, he had imagined what it had to feel like. Had believed that he knew what emotions were evoked. But Jackson realized now that he hadn't even come close.

There was absolutely no way he could have known what holding a child in his arms within moments of its birth would actually feel like. Not without experiencing it first-hand.

When the delivery room nurse handed him the tiny, squalling bit of humanity, it was like holding a piece of the future in his arms.

Or maybe it was more like catching a star that had fallen out of the sky and for one brief shining moment, being allowed to examine it while it shimmered in the palm of his hand.

It was all that and more. So much more so that he couldn't even begin to describe it. Words failed him.

And the child wasn't even his. But for that same brief

moment, he could pretend that it was. Pretend and believe that Joshua was really his child. His and Mallory's.

Jackson looked toward Mallory. Their eyes met and held in silent communion above this newly minted Californian's tiny head. They'd barely had enough time to reach the delivery room and position themselves before the entire process was all over. The pain, the screaming and the wonder, all over in a little more than the blink of an eye. Fifteen minutes after he had put on the green livery in the locker room, Jackson was holding Mallory's son in his arms.

He hadn't even really had an opportunity to coach her, which was just as well because he would have been completely out of his element. Not too long ago, a friend of his had cornered him with tales of delivery room horrors. Jackson was relieved that none of that had come to pass. Relieved for himself and especially for Mallory. The idea that she would have had to endure that level of pain was completely repugnant to him.

The infant squirmed in his arms. Jackson looked down at the small, puckered face.

"He looks like my grandfather," he commented with a laugh.

With no effort, Jackson could picture the old man across the span of time. He was sitting at the breakfast table, reading the morning stock reports and frowning so deeply that it made an eight-year-old boy think the lines were indelible. After a time, they had been.

Well, that was a breeze. Sheila smiled as she undid her mask. The last few deliveries she'd attended had been particularly long and difficult. It was a relief when one went the other way.

"I'd say that had to be one of the fastest deliveries I've ever had the pleasure to oversee." She nodded at Mallory. "I think you might have even set a hospital record." Humor crinkled in her sapphire blue eyes as she squeezed Mallory's hand. "You did good, Mallory. You did real good." Because her own time was quickly drawing near, Sheila couldn't help adding, "I only hope that my delivery goes as well as yours did."

Sheila didn't add that her fondest hope was for the father of her baby to suddenly appear beside her the way Jackson had with Mallory. She was a practical woman who didn't deal in fantasies and that particular dream went beyond the realm of wishes and well into the field of fantasy.

She roused herself. She'd gone into this situation with her eyes wide open, even though the outcome hadn't been planned and she was adult enough to handle the consequences. There were lots of single mothers out there and she was going to join them soon.

He certainly looked proud, she thought, watching Jackson. Behind him, Sheila saw the delivery room nurse waiting with a patient expression on her face. Sheila nudged Jackson gently.

He looked at the doctor in surprise. For a second, he'd forgotten that there was anyone else in the room besides him and the baby he held.

"I think we need to get this young man spruced up a bit so that he's presentable when he's brought out to join his peers in the nursery." Sheila saw Mallory reaching out to touch the tiny foot that was peeking out from beneath Jackson's arm. A germ of separation syndrome was already setting in. "Don't worry," she assured Mallory, "he'll be back before you know it."

Mallory could only nod. She was too exhausted and too emotional right now to say anything. There were too many emotions running helter-skelter through her, colliding with each other like skaters on in-line skates for the first time.

She'd had a son today.

More than that, she'd gotten the opportunity to see Jackson holding their child. She never thought that would happen. Mallory felt moisture on her lashes and didn't know if she was crying, or still perspiring. But she did know that she was twelve steps beyond being utterly overwhelmed.

"He looks so tiny," Jackson commented as he surrendered the infant to the nurse.

The baby felt as if he weighed next to nothing, yet the absence of his tiny body created an instant, incredible dearth in Jackson's arms.

"Not really. And he'll be growing very fast," Sheila said. The infant let out a lusty yell three times his size just as the nurse disappeared with him through the doorway. Sheila grinned as the door closed behind them. "He's feisty. You'll probably have your hands full," she added with a soft laugh.

She glanced at the clock on the far wall. So much for grabbing a quick lunch, she mused. It was almost two. Time for office hours to resume. "Well, I still have pregnant women to see to." She stopped beside the delivery table. "You worked that right into a nice niche, Mallory. I wish all my patients were this accommodating." Sheila nodded to the other nurse who stood ready to wheel Mallory into the recovery room. "I'll come by to look in on you tonight," she promised.

The next moment, Sheila was gone from the room with more grace and agility than, in Jackson's opinion, a woman in her condition would normally display.

Following on the doctor's heels, Jackson held the swinging doors open for the nurse as the woman pushed Mallory's gurney through and out into the hall.

Now what? For one of the few times in his life, Jackson Cain felt awkward. He fell into step beside the gurney as the nurse wheeled Mallory down the hall to the recovery room. He wanted to hold her hand, to somehow bond with her at this moment of wonder, but he restrained himself. It really wasn't his moment to share. It belonged to another man.

His eyes met Mallory's. He said the first words that came into his head. "I guess the doctor thinks he's mine."

Mallory was far too exhausted to debate the situation or to attempt to lie to him about it. She'd come up with something later, when her head was clearer.

"Natural mistake," she murmured.

All of it, she thought, her mind swirling around in a murky haze that was becoming progressively darker and more encompassing. All of it had been just a natural mistake. Loving Jackson had been a mistake....

No, no it hadn't. She had a son, a beautiful, tiny son. Whatever had been involved in creating him could never be thought of as a mistake....

Mallory fell asleep before she ever heard Jackson's response.

He stood just before the double doors, locked out. Beyond them lay the recovery room and Mallory. The nurse had assured him that Mallory would be in her room within an hour. His obligations to her, such as they were, were over. He was free to leave.

He didn't.

There was no earthly reason to remain. But he did.

Shoving his hands into his pockets, he walked down the hall to the elevators.

He wasn't quite sure what to do with himself right now, or how to deal with the feelings that were bouncing around inside of him like overheated, charged popcorn kernels. He hadn't even checked into a hotel yet. Seeing Mallory had been his first priority when he arrived in Newport Beach.

And now that he had, everything had been turned upside down.

A cryptic smile lifted the corners of his mouth as he pressed for the elevator. Mallory had always had that sort of effect on him. He'd always enjoyed the company of beautiful women. But it had always been just that, company. An interesting way to while away the evening or the weekend, nothing more. Staying with one woman had never been on his agenda. Not for him was a monogamous union sealed for all time because of appearances. He wasn't about to be buried alive within a sham, an empty shell of what had once been a thriving relationship. Living a sham might have been all right for his parents, but he wasn't his parents.

And then came Mallory and all the carefully measured rules he'd laid down for himself had become distorted. When he had finally forced himself to leave her for his own self-preservation, Jackson had congratulated himself heartily on bailing out just in time.

Or had he?

The victory had felt a little hollow even then. Now it was not only hollow, but brittle as well.

In desperate need of a cup of coffee, Jackson found his way down to the basement level cafeteria. He bought himself a container of inky black liquid and a large glazed bear claw, and found a table in the corner, out of the way of the main foot traffic. He needed some time alone to think. Maybe the coffee would help him see things more clearly.

Two refills later, the bear claw sat untouched, a sticky clump of sugar and dough, and his emotions were just as tangled as before. For the first time in his life, Jackson had come face-to-face with a side of himself he didn't care for. He'd been jealous of Steven. *Was* jealous of Steven. Jealousy had risen up within him like a malignant growth he had no idea how to begin to cut out.

Being wired with three cups of caffeine didn't exactly help matters either.

This was his own fault, he mused, pushing the bear claw farther away on the table. If he hadn't left, none of this would have happened. But when he'd left, he thought he'd left for good. How was he to know making love with Mallory came under the heading of Addiction? There'd been no way to foretell that the memory of warm, pleasure-filled nights humming through his brain would lure him back here like a siren's song.

And now he'd returned only in time to find her giving birth to some other man's child.

The chair legs scraped along the vinyl-covered floor as he

pushed it back and rose abruptly. He couldn't very well have expected Mallory just to sit, pining away for him in some corner like a lovesick adolescent. This wasn't seventeenth century England. He wasn't some brooding bard in a stiff collar and tights, roaming through a castle while he created couplets in his head. And Mallory wasn't some delicate flower, given to vapors.

He laughed to himself at the image, knowing what Mallory would have had to say about it. She was the complete opposite of a shrinking violet, a vibrant, beautiful woman with a zest for life and the right to seize it.

But did she have to seize it quite so damn quickly? he thought grudgingly as he found his way back to the elevators.

Getting in, he pushed the button for the first floor. He had a few more loose ends to tie up before he hit the road back to New York.

Sleeping. She was sleeping, Mallory realized as the blanketing haze slowly lifted from her brain. As it left, the pain returned with spiky edges. Her body was aching all over. Was she going into labor? No, wait, she'd done that already, hadn't she?

Or had she just dreamed it all? The baby, Jackson returning, had it all been just another dream, like all the other ones?

Even before she opened her eyes, Mallory's hand spread tentatively out over her abdomen. It was flat, or at least flatter. The swollen, taut-skinned mound was a thing of the past. She'd had the baby. It wasn't a dream. She'd had a son.

Joshua, she thought, remembering.

A fond ache spilled through her as she remembered everything. Was he here, in her room? Had they left her baby in a bassinet beside her bed?

Mallory forced her lids open. With effort, she tried to focus on her surroundings. She knew she was supposed to be in a hospital room, but it looked way too large and too homey to qualify. It was more like a guest room in some-one's house. Like Dorothy after her house had dropped in Oz, Mallory felt completely disoriented.

Where *was* she? And how long had she been asleep?

Confused, Mallory pulled her elbows in against her sides and tried to prop herself up into a sitting position. She'd only partially succeeded when she felt a restraining hand on her arm.

"Hey, take it easy."

Her heart thudded against her ribs. She hadn't dreamed it. Jackson *had* returned.

"Jackson," she breathed as she turned her head toward him. Seeing him, she felt delirious all over again. Why did he have to come back and ruin everything? She was over him. Over.

The hell she was.

The way she said his name still sent a shiver down his spine, he thought.

"Yeah, it's me." Smiling, he took her hand. Mallory still looked pale. Was that normal? "How are you feeling?"

"Wobbly." And even more so with him holding her hand. She pulled it away and looked around the room. "Where am I?"

Jackson drew the easy chair over to her bed and sat down. He'd been sitting in it for over half an hour, just watching her sleep, trying to come up with answers. All he'd suc-ceeded in doing was creating more questions for himself.

"In the hospital."

It certainly didn't look like any hospital room she had ever seen. "But the room—"

The private room was a cut and a half above the others on the floor, but at the price he was paying, he thought, it should be.

"I had you upgraded," he told her with a grin. "It's all paid for." It was the very least he could do. "Consider it my 'birthday' present to the baby. I thought you and he might want to be alone.''

She didn't want to be indebted to Jackson, but then, she probably always would be, Mallory amended, seeing as how he had given her the son she intended to cherish and love with all her heart. She might as well make the most of it.

''That's very nice of you.''

Mallory blew out a breath and dragged a hand through her hair. She had to look like a mess. She remembered that he'd been there during the delivery and bit back her embarrassment. Instead, she concentrated on the positive side. She'd needed someone and Jackson had been there for her.

''You didn't really have to stay for the delivery.'' Her eyes touched his. ''Thanks.''

He shrugged carelessly. Gratitude was something he didn't assimilate easily. ''I didn't have much choice. Your doctor practically railroaded me into the delivery room. She always that strong willed?''

So much for attributing noble sentiments to him, Mallory thought. In answer to his question, she lifted a shoulder and let it drop.

''Not with me.'' Mallory forced herself to look past his head and not at him. ''She obviously mistook you for the father and probably thought you just needed a little coaxing.''

Mallory fervently hoped Sheila hadn't said anything to him about what she had told the woman at the start of her pregnancy. Stunned, upset, the whole story had just come pouring out of her. It had all happened in a moment of weakness. Though everyone turned to Mallory with their problems and looked to her for guidance, she was by nature closemouthed when it came to her own life. It was just that the news of her pregnancy, coming on the heels of Jackson's abrupt departure, had caught her completely unprepared and left her feeling vulnerable.

She didn't want Jackson knowing that Joshua was his son. All her little fantasies notwithstanding, Mallory had already made up her mind that she wasn't going to tell Jackson that he was the father. Above all else, she didn't want Jackson feeling obligated to provide for her. She didn't want anything from him that he felt he *had* to give.

He'd made it perfectly clear to her when he left that he wasn't the type to commit. If he knew the baby was his, she doubted very much that the knowledge would make him change his Bohemian life-style. Financially, she knew he would provide for the boy. Even without his lucrative income as a bestselling author of spine-tingling whodunits, he was more than comfortably well off.

It didn't matter. She didn't want his money. Mallory could more than adequately provide for her baby and herself. What she wanted from Jackson was his heart, something he wasn't about to give. There was no way Jackson would ever marry her. He valued his freedom too much. He'd told her so in words as well as actions.

It would only confuse Joshua to have his father whimsically flittering in and out of his life, disrupting it each time he turned up.

Just the way he'd disrupted her life now by returning to her.

Jackson thought he'd come to terms with his jealousy in the cafeteria. But here it was again, rising up full-bodied and ugly.

With effort, he banked it down. "Speaking of his father, just where is *Steven* supposed to be? Our earlier conversation was rather abruptly curtailed."

Mallory shifted uncomfortably. "Why do you want to know?"

Jackson gave his own interpretation to her reticence. She was afraid he was going to do something to her lover. Did she think so little of him?

"Don't worry, Mallory, I don't intend to hurt him. I just thought that you'd want him to know." He looked at the telephone next to her bed. "I could call him for you."

In the car, on the way over, she'd thought that perhaps Jackson was a little jealous of the man she'd made up, jealous of the affection she'd given him. Now she realized that it was only wishful thinking on her part. He seemed almost eager to push the two of them together.

He didn't care at all about her. But then, she already knew that, she reminded herself with a bitter pang.

"Of course I want him to know," she answered indignantly. "But you can't call him."

Her mind raced around for a plausible excuse. She thought of Ursula. Ursula Sanchez was a woman who worked in her office. Mallory had spent her entire lunch hour comforting Ursula yesterday. Ursula's husband had just left on an extended business trip and she was upset because there was no way she could communicate with him.

"There're no phones," she added almost triumphantly.

He looked at her, unconvinced and confused. "Just exactly where is he?"

"Alaska." She hoped Jackson wouldn't ask her where in Alaska. She couldn't remember the name of the city Ursula had mentioned.

Jackson cocked his brow. "Last I heard, Alaska's pretty civilized. They've had phone service for at least a week and a half now."

Mallory looked down at her blanket. Fingers spread wide, she smoothed it out along her legs. "Not where he is."

Jackson studied her face carefully. Something just didn't sound right. Or maybe it was just wishful thinking on his part. "Just what is it that this Steven of yours does for a living?"

"He's a petroleum engineer." Afraid of any more questions, she went on the offensive. "Why all these questions?"

The shrug was a little too casual, his manner a little too blasé. "I'm just curious about the man who replaced me."

Mallory pressed the control button on her bed, raising the headboard so that their eyes were almost level. The throbbing pain in her body took a back seat to the one in her heart.

"He didn't replace you, Jackson. You vacated the spot, remember?" She attempted to keep the bitter edge out of her voice. It wasn't a completely successful effort. "As I recall, you couldn't leave it fast enough."

She was absolutely right and he didn't want to go over that now. "Let's not debate semantics, Mallory. I'm just trying to be helpful." His tone was light, belying his feelings. "Are you sure I can't reach Steven for you?"

She raised her chin and replied with dignity, "I'm sure."

He couldn't help hating the man who had held her, who had made love with her in his stead. If it was unreasonable, that was beside the point. Jackson had never regretted anything he'd ever done before. He was filled with regret now.

He stared out the window, trying to calm the inner turmoil he felt. The view of the ocean from the fifth story window was soothing.

It didn't help.

"Do you two live together?" he asked in a low, quiet voice.

The question, coming out of the blue, caught her at a disadvantage. "No. Yes." She scowled, quickly fabricating a cover story in her mind. God, but this was tiring. Why didn't he just go and leave her alone? "Sort of."

This was beginning to sound stranger and stranger. Amused, he grinned at her. "I always did like multiple choice."

He was laughing at her. Damn him, anyway. "I'm a little muddled, okay? In case you don't remember, I just gave birth. I didn't have time to bone up for an interrogation."

He took her hand, but she pulled it away again. "That's the beauty of interrogations, Mallory. You can't bone up for them. They're supposed to be spontaneous." And if this was an interrogation, it was creating more questions than it was answering.

"Like chaos," she commented. Mallory crossed her arms in front of her. "All right, I've got a question of my own."

Jackson leaned back in his chair, looking far too smug for her liking. "Shoot."

*Don't tempt me.* "Just why did you come back here?" And why now, of all times?

He wanted to tell her that he was here because of her, because she'd haunted his days and his nights and he knew he wasn't going to have any peace until he saw her again. But that was before he'd discovered that she belonged to someone else. A man had his pride, even if it had caused him to make a major mistake.

"I'm gathering data for another book about the coast. I started making preliminary notes and found a few gaps in my memory." He figured it was an explanation she would accept, and in part, it was true. He'd put in a little time visiting locales during the day. It turned out to be more for nostalgic reasons than anything else.

"I'm sure they'll match the ones in your head just splendidly," she murmured.

He laughed, tickled by her retort. She was beginning to sound like her feisty self again. A feisty woman he'd fallen hard for because she gave as good as she got. "Maybe. Anyway, I need a place to crash." He took a chance. "Mind if I stay with you?"

She stared at him, stunned. What "need"? The man could have bought his own hotel if he wanted to. Belatedly, she remembered how much he hated the artificial atmosphere hotels created. But that still didn't mean she had to take him in.

"Yes, I mind." Did he think he could come waltzing back into her life just like that? She'd just told him that she was involved in a relationship and had borne another man's child. Just how fatal did he think his charm was? "God, Jackson, when they were handing out gall, you must have gone back for thirds."

He held his hand up knowing that once she got going it was hard to get a word in edgewise. "Now hear me out. It only seems logical. You're going to need a helping hand with the baby—"

Now that was *really* reaching. "Since when did you become good with kids?"

He looked at her innocently. "It's a learning thing," he said smoothly. "Two inexperienced people are better than one." Expertly, Jackson hit her where she lived. "You're going to want to sleep in a couple of mornings—" She was as far from a morning person as he was from being the first man on Mars.

Mallory's mouth curved in a smirk. "Somehow, I just can't picture you breast-feeding."

Jackson remained unfazed. "We'll work something out." He paused for effect, then added nonchalantly, "Unless of course Steven's due back and this is his week to 'sort of' live with you."

Her eyes narrowed. She didn't appreciate him ridiculing her. Without a clue as to how long Jackson intended to remain in Newport, she stretched the thin fabric she'd woven a little further.

"He's not going to be back for another three weeks." There, that should cover all contingencies. Jackson and his wandering feet would be long gone by the time three weeks were up.

This was making less and less sense to him. How could Mallory love a man who had such little regard for her as to leave when she was so close to her due date? The fact that he was setting standards for the missing man that he didn't meet himself was something Jackson chose not to dwell on.

"He left you for that long when you're expecting?"

Caught up in the lie, Mallory took umbrage for the man she'd created. "He didn't have a choice and besides, I was due at the end of March, not the beginning." She looked at Jackson pointedly. "And I would have probably delivered close to my due date if you hadn't shown up when and the way that you did."

Her words stung him more than he would have imagined. "Oh, so now it's my fault?"

"Yes." A lot of things were his fault. Most prominently, the way she was feeling in her head. "Stress sometimes induces labor."

He probably deserved this and more, but it didn't make it any easier to take. "And I come under the heading of stress?"

She'd hurt him, she realized. Why didn't that feel good? It should have.

"Yes," Mallory said quietly. "You do."

A retort hovered on his lips, born of frustration and anger, both of which were aimed at himself.

Jackson swallowed the retort and then nodded. "Maybe you're right. If you are, I'm sorry." His hand closed over hers. It was time to leave. He'd overstayed as it was. "I'm glad everything turned out all right with the baby."

Exits were his specialty. He'd managed them time and again, whenever a situation got a little too warm, a little too close for comfort. This time, though, he found it difficult.

Still, he never remained where he wasn't wanted. Jackson leaned over Mallory's bed. Lightly, he brushed his lips over hers. Long tentacles of desire instantly penetrated, hooking onto him. Helpless, he lingered a moment longer, wishing it could be forever. He felt her catch her breath, then exhale. It flittered over his face, exciting him, reminding him of what he had lost.

God, but he missed her.

"Tell this Steven character that if he doesn't treat you right, he'll have me to answer to." His eyes washed over her face, caressing it one last time. "You're a very special woman, Mallory. You deserve the best." He looked at her closely. Her eyes were shimmering. "Are you crying?"

Yes, she was, but she wasn't about to admit it to him. "Allergies," she murmured, sniffling.

She didn't have any as far as he knew, but he let it ride. He merely nodded, as if he believed her. "Better have them give you something for them."

With that, he turned and began to walk away.

She was a fool, Mallory thought, a damn fool. But there was something about his retreating back that pricked at her heart.

That, and the fact that even though the kiss had been chaste by any definition, it still managed to stir things up within her. Things she'd been so certain that she had sealed away for good. Jackson Cain had been the only man she'd ever loved.

And damn if she still didn't.

Mallory licked her bottom lip, debating. She tasted his mouth. It wasn't fair, she thought. It wasn't fair to feel like this about a man who'd dumped her.

From nowhere, a thought occurred to her. Why not make him regret it? Why not make him regret just what he walked out on? And then, when he did, hold it out of his reach? It would serve him right.

A slow smile curved her mouth. Yes, it would serve him right.

"Jackson," she called after him.

He stopped just shy of the door, his hand on the jamb. "Yes?"

"Maybe you can stay. Just for a few days," she added quickly when he turned around to look at her. If she sounded eager, his suspicions would be aroused.

"Really? You're sure?"

"Yes," she answered. When he looked at her, she felt her pulse jump hard enough to make a showing on the Richter scale. She was going to have to watch that, she admonished herself. "I'm sure."

# Four

―――

"**D**on't argue with me, Ursula, just do it. All right?" Mallory shifted the telephone to her other ear. She didn't have much time. Jackson would be by at any minute to pick her up. The doctor had left orders to discharge her an hour ago. She had to get this in motion before he arrived. "Please?"

There was a pause on the other end of the line, as if Ursula were trying to find some hidden meaning in what Mallory had asked her to do.

"Let me get this straight. You want me to buy you four long-sleeved men's shirts and underwear."

"Yes." Mallory kept her eyes on the door. "No, wait, make it half a dozen."

That sounded better. After all, Steven wasn't supposed to be living with her, just spending the night once in a while. That meant he'd have to have at least a reasonable amount of things at her house.

Ursula played along, though she still sounded bewildered. "Any particular color or size?"

"I don't know. Briefs." All she could think of was Jackson and what he would wear. But she didn't want Steven to be like Jackson. He had to be different. Unique. "Use your judgment, Ursula." She banked down her irritation. It wasn't Ursula's fault she was in this situation. "You're the one with a husband."

There was a light chuckle on the other end of the line. "I think you have this a little backward, Mallory. First you get the husband, then you get the clothes for his wardrobe."

Ursula's attempt at humor passed right over her. This was an emergency. She didn't need jokes, she needed someone who could carry out her instructions. Quickly.

"I'm not filling a hope chest, Ursula. I need you to get these things so that I can convince someone that there's a man in my life."

Ursula felt more confused than ever. Mallory was too free spirited to worry about conventional behavior. "I think the baby might do a better job of that than underwear."

Mallory automatically shook her head in response. "Not this man. He needs more proof." She had to convince Jackson that Steven existed and that he was the father of her baby. Otherwise, Jackson would come to the only other logical conclusion. That Joshua was his and that would be disastrous. "Ursula, I really need this favor, and I need it done now. Okay?"

Ursula sighed, indicating that it definitely was *not* okay as far as she understood the matter.

"All right, how do I get the props over to your place? I'm assuming you want them there before you come home from the hospital."

"Exactly. That gives you about an hour, no more." She heard Ursula groan. "I'm sorry, but this really is important."

She'd only thought of the added touch a few minutes ago. The more ammunition she had at her disposal, the better. If Jackson saw no male trappings at all, he might get suspicious and start asking questions. And if seeing them made him jealous, well, so much the better.

It was too soon to be congratulating herself. Ursula was going to have to get in before she could put things away, she reminded herself. "I've got a spare key to my house in my middle drawer in the office. It's mixed in with the paper clips."

There was silence as Ursula went to check. "Got it. No one would have ever thought of looking there," she quipped.

"You didn't," Mallory pointed out.

Ursula only sighed again. "Does this mystery man of yours wear pants?"

Pants. She'd forgotten all about that. "Good point. Buy a couple of those while you're at it. Thirty-two long," she added for good measure. "I'll pay you back as soon as I see you, I promise." She realized she was asking a lot of Ursula. "Or I could mail you a check." That would probably be faster.

"I'm not worried about the money, Mallory. I am, however, worried about you." Ursula's voice became concerned. "Just how many painkillers are they giving you at the hospital?"

Mallory thought of the way Jackson still affected her. Of the way she just had to look up into his eyes to have all the old feelings come rushing back with a vengeance. And she was determined not to let him overwhelm her. He'd had no right to treat her that way. She was going to pay him back for that and, she hoped, finally succeed in getting him out of her blood for good.

"Not nearly enough, Ursula, not nearly enough." She glanced at the clock. "Now hurry, please. I'm going home this afternoon and I need to have all those things put away before I get there."

The plot was thickening. "You want me to put them away?"

"Of course I want you to put them away." Agitation filled her voice. "That's the whole point. He can't come in to see them just sitting there in a bag. He'll know that I had someone buy them."

Ursula's flagging attention was suddenly sparked. *"He?"*

She didn't have time to get into it and even if she did, she didn't want to. "Never mind, it's a very long story."

Ursula gave no indication of taking the hint. "I'm on lunch—"

Ursula collected stories about other people's lives like some people collected magazines. Mallory was in no mood to satisfy her curiosity. "Great, then you can hurry out and buy those clothes for me."

Disappointment threaded through the deep sigh. "'Bye, Mallory. I sure hope you know what you're doing."

"So do I," Mallory murmured under her breath as she heard Ursula break the connection. "Oh God, so do I."

There was no time to ponder the wisdom of getting so deeply imbedded in the lie she'd spun for herself. Jackson walked in just as she was reaching over to replace the receiver into the cradle.

The receiver slipped from her fingers and landed on the telephone with a thud. She hardly noticed.

"Hi." He flashed her a smile and noted with pleasure that her attention was on the bouquet of yellow tea roses he had in his hand, and the teddy bear that was tucked under his arm.

Mallory looked amazed, and then to his surprise, she began to laugh.

The sound went straight to his gut, stirring him. Before he could stop himself, he leaned over and brushed a kiss on her lips. It only had him wanting more. "What are you laughing at?"

The laughter died as soon as his mouth touched hers. It brought back too many memories, too many emotions. Damn it, how could she make him believe she was involved with another man if he saw he could shake her up with just a simple kiss? Mallory had to concentrate to answer his question.

"I never pictured you with a teddy bear." Her eyes swept over the bouquet. He'd never brought her flowers before. It didn't go with his image. "Or flowers for that matter."

He'd just barely touched her lips, yet he could still taste her flavor. And it made him remember another time, another place. In his mind's eye he could see her, nude upon his bed, her skin golden, caressed by candlelight. She moved invitingly, warm and supple under his hand.

He blinked, chasing away the memory. But it hovered just within reach, waiting to torment him again.

"Maybe I've changed."

"Maybe."

It would take more than flowers to convince her of that. Much more. More than she knew he could give. She couldn't let herself start believing in the impossible. She'd only wind up torturing herself.

"You get first choice." He presented both to her. "Flowers or teddy bear."

She took the bouquet from him. "I'd better let Josh have the teddy bear. He might want to suck on the flowers."

Her son, she'd already noted with pleasure, had a very deep-rooted sucking instinct. He'd taken to her breast with no hesitation whatsoever.

A lot like his father, she thought involuntarily, her eyes rising to Jackson's.

"You remembered." She'd always loved the scent of roses. She took a deep breath and let the fragrance invade her senses. "Or was that just an accident?"

Jackson tucked the teddy bear in the far corner of the bassinet. He could have sworn that the baby was staring at the fuzzy stuffed animal.

"No accident," he told her.

*Not like Joshua,* she thought. *But if ever there was a wonderful accident, it was Joshua.*

Something was going on just behind her eyes. Something that involved him. "What?" Jackson coaxed.

*Oh no, not that easily.* She wasn't about to let the secret go.

"Nothing," Mallory replied, swinging her legs off the bed. "Just thinking."

He watched as Mallory smoothed her skirt over her legs. Jackson had trouble keeping his mind on the subject. She had legs that could make a man's mouth water and bring him to his knees.

"About?"

She looked toward the bassinet. The teddy bear was larger than Joshua. But not for long. In no time at all, Joshua would be out, playing, running and getting into mischief.

"About what an overwhelming responsibility it is to have a son." Rising, she crossed to the bassinet. Very gently, she tucked the cotton blanket around the tiny form. "I'm going to have to make sure he's raised right and that he learns how to respect women from the very beginning," she vowed softly.

Jackson came up behind her. He wondered if she had intended for her words to sting. They did.

A bittersweet smile played on his lips. "I guess then you wouldn't want me to be giving him any pointers."

Mallory closed her eyes, trying to steel herself off from his presence. With effort, she forced a smile. There was no point in letting him know how much she'd been hurt. Nothing would change if he knew, and some things were best kept secret.

"Not until he's thirty," she replied cheerfully.

Jackson ran his hands along her arms, remembering another time, another place. "I've missed you, Mallory," he said softly.

*No, you didn't. You would have returned a lot sooner if you had.*

She stiffened under his touch. Pulling back, she swung around to face him. Her expression was unreadable, but her eyes implored him to keep his distance.

"Don't. If you want to come over and stay a few days at my place, you're welcome to do so. But there are going to have to be ground rules." She had to lay them down immediately. The last thing she needed was to have him undo her like this.

Mallory held her hands up in front of her to prevent him from touching her again. "We're just friends, got that?"

He looked into her eyes. "We were more than just friends."

Yes, they had been, but he had put a stop to it when he left. She wasn't about to be sucked into that scenario again, wasn't going to start spinning dreams that had no hope of coming true. She wasn't a complete idiot. She learned from her mistakes.

"That was then, this is now. I have a baby and a—" She hesitated just a moment. "A significant other in my life. I want your word that you'll behave."

That all depended on your definition of *behave,* Jackson mused. There was something still very much alive between them. If there hadn't been, she wouldn't have agreed to his staying with her. She wouldn't be looking at him the way she was now.

Inclining his head, Jackson put his hand out to her. "I'll behave."

Hesitantly, she slipped her hand into his, wondering if she *did* know what she was doing. The so-called truce didn't make her feel any better. "Why don't I believe you?"

"You're too cautious?" he offered.

"Or gullible," she countered.

Before she could stop him, he cupped her cheek, then dropped his hand to his side of his own volition. "You were never gullible, Mallory."

*Oh, yes I was.* Mallory looked away.

Jackson looked down at Joshua. The baby had fallen asleep. She'd dressed him in a yellow crochet jacket with a matching hat. The same shade of yellow as the flowers he had brought to her. "Well, it looks like he's all set to leave."

Mallory had finished getting Joshua dressed just before she'd called Ursula. She'd been dressed ever since the doctor had left, eager to leave the hospital and get on with her life as a new mother. Nothing was going to spoil this for her.

She toyed with the edge of Joshua's blanket. He looked so tiny, lying there. "Doesn't take much to get a baby ready."

Jackson shoved his hands into his back pockets to keep from reaching for Mallory again. He had this overwhelming urge to kiss her, really kiss her, the way they both deserved, unforeseen circumstances not withstanding.

He grinned. "As I recall, you could get dressed really fast yourself."

One look into his eyes and Mallory knew exactly what he was referring to. The time when he'd talked her into making love in a vacated Open House she was sitting in. The house had been on the market for weeks and the owner had relocated to Florida. The day had dragged by without a single prospective buyer showing up to look at the house. Jackson had dropped by just before she was about to close up.

Mallory could remember it as clearly as if it had happened only moments ago. Just remembering heated her blood....

"Hi, Gorgeous." Closing the front door deliberately, he crossed to her and nuzzled her neck.

She was about to protest that the door was supposed to remain open to entice clients. But she was being enticed herself. As he held her to him, his hand was lightly brushing along her breast.

The reaction was instantaneous, even though this was neither the time nor the place for yearnings like this. But then, Jackson had a way of sweeping away things like propriety. Just being with him was exciting.

She fought for a clear head. It was a struggle doomed from the start. "What are you doing here? I thought you had work to do." She knew how important his work was to him and he'd complained, just this morning, that he was far behind his own schedule.

"I did. I do." Jackson shrugged carelessly, dismissing the question. "I'd rather be here, with you. Taking tiny bites out of your neck." To prove it, he skimmed just his teeth along her throat, then marked the path with the tip of his tongue.

Mallory shivered. Her knees were growing weak. And she knew where this was leading. Where it always seemed to lead whenever they were around one another. Not that she didn't want it to, but this was far too public a place to give in to the urges that were suddenly hammering within her.

"Does this place have a bedroom?" She felt his question gliding along her throat, sending shivers along her body. The pit of her stomach tightened.

"Yes." She could hardly squeeze the word out.

Jackson took her hand in his, urging her toward the stairs. "Show me."

Mallory didn't remember walking up the stairs. She brought him into the master bedroom searching for the strength to refuse him. To refuse herself. She could only muster the most cursory attempt.

"Jackson, we can't do this," she protested as he took her into his arms.

The smile in his eyes was wicked as he cupped her face in his hand. Ever so lightly, he brushed his thumb along her lower lip, making her tremble in anticipation.

"Yes, we can," he whispered. "Watch."

"Jackson." It was a losing battle. Especially since even she wasn't on her own side. "I'm showing a house."

"And what a lovely house it is." His mouth curved as he unbuttoned her blouse one agonizing button at a time.

She wanted to stop him, but her fingers weren't doing what they were supposed to be doing. They were limp, damp, while her mouth felt as dry as cotton. "People will be coming—"

His smile said he knew better. "It's almost time to close up." Slipping her blouse from her shoulders, he pressed a kiss to each one. His breath was hot along her arms. "And it's raining." Fingers tangling with the straps of her bra, he tugged them down the same path. "Rain always makes me feel sexy."

His eyes were holding her, loving her. Every solid thing within her was turning to liquid and quickly turning to molten lava. She wasn't even sure she was breathing. If she was, it was only sporadically.

"Does it make you feel sexy?"

Jackson ended his question by opening the clasp on her bra. The cups slid from her breasts. He covered them with his palms and gently massaged.

Mallory groaned. She was miles passed sexy, running straight into wanton. "Looking at a butterfly collection with you makes me feel sexy."

He laughed then. The deep, throaty sound wove under her skin, deciding the verdict of the battle she'd only halfheartedly fought.

Unable to resist, she surrendered. With hands that trembled, she worked at divesting him of his clothing. She almost ripped off two of his buttons.

He laughed as the shirt landed in a heap over her blouse. "Why, what's your hurry?"

She saw his eyes flutter just a little as she tugged his jeans from his hips.

Mallory moistened her lips. "Someone might come."

Jackson stepped out of the jeans at his feet. And into her heart. With a swift motion, he removed her skirt and pulled her to him, heat blending with heat.

"Doubtful." He sounded so sure, it almost succeeded in putting her mind at ease. "But that just adds spice." His hands were on her skin, beneath her panties. And then even they were gone. "You know what spice is, don't you Mallory?"

Easing her down on the bed, he was over her now, his body blanketing hers. Teasing hers. She thought she was going to burst into flame. "What?"

His tongue outlined her mouth before he answered. "What I find on your lips."

There'd been no more words then, just a passionate tangling of emotions, of bodies and such wondrous ecstasy that she forgot everything else but Jackson. Everything else, but the needs that could be fulfilled by him. Only him.

He caressed, stroked, teased, as if they had all day. All night. She twisted and turned beneath him, absorbing every nuance and building on it. Wanting more. Needing more.

"Now," she cried, desperately. "Now."

Arching, she stifled a cry as he sheathed himself within her. The pace was breathtakingly fast. If she had been a cauldron, she would have boiled over.

Mallory clung to him when it was over, wishing they were back in her bed where this would be only a prelude to a night of loving.

Sliding off, Jackson gathered her against him. She could feel his heart beating as wildly as hers. It comforted her, made her feel loved and contented.

Until she heard the front door opening and closing.

"Hello, is anyone here?" someone called from the first floor.

Bolting upright, she'd stared at Jackson, horror stricken.

He looked unfazed, amused. "My mistake."

Heart hammering, Mallory grabbed her clothes. "Get dressed," she hissed.

He did as she asked, obviously enjoying the complication. "You could always say I was a life-sized statue that came with the place," he teased.

As if she'd ever let anyone else have him. "Not on your life."

* * *

It had taken her exactly two minutes flat to pull on all her clothes and become presentable enough to greet the couple. Her enthusiasm and energy level had been so charged, she'd wound up selling the house to them.

She could still hear Jackson laughing the entire drive home.

Mallory distanced herself from the memory. It took effort. "That will be rule number one." She held up one finger for emphasis. "No reminiscing."

Reminiscing was an integral part of the plan that was forming in his mind.

"Oh, but—" Jackson reached for her hand.

She quickly pulled it back, out of range. "Rule number two, no touching."

He didn't think she'd adhere to that rule, but for now, he raised his hands in blatant surrender. "Then I guess kissing would be out of the question."

No, no kissing. He'd shown her just how vulnerable she still was around him. And how vulnerable she would always probably be. Like malaria, he would never be out of her system completely, but she could definitely employ whatever safeguards against him that she could. She knew she had to be able to withstand being around him in order to face herself.

And then she could tell him to go to hell and get away from her.

"Absolutely."

He curtailed the urge to toy with her hair. Instead, he looked down at the sleeping infant. "Can I hold the baby?"

Mallory swallowed. There was no earthly reason why her mouth felt so dry. She nodded in reply. "Holding the baby will be fine."

Mischief she was well acquainted with danced in his eyes. She felt as if he were silently putting her on notice. Two could play that game, she thought, digging in. Before she was finished, she'd have him on his knees, begging her to take him back.

That was when she intended to step all over his heart, the way he had on hers.

"It's a start," he murmured.

Jackson reached into the bassinet and picked up the infant. It was amazing, he mused, how easily the baby seemed to fit into the crook of his arm. It was almost as if Joshua had been created with just the right measurements.

He slanted a glance toward Mallory. She was hovering, he thought. Probably thought he was going to drop Josh. "Still looks like my grandfather."

Telling herself to relax, she smiled. "All babies look like somebody's grandfather. It's that little old man look they have about them."

She hoped he wouldn't extrapolate on the resemblance any further. Maybe she was being unduly nervous, but Joshua looked exactly like a photograph Jackson had showed her of himself as a baby. He had the same gaunt features, the same olive complexion, while she was fair enough to have seven little men following her wherever she went. Would he notice that?

Crossing back to the bed, Mallory found the buzzer and rang for the nurse. Was she asking for trouble, letting him stay with her?

Probably. Mallory pressed her lips together as she turned around to look at Jackson. Very probably. But she was just going to have to deal with that. And remember her goal. To make him regret leaving her. If at any time during his visit she felt the urge to tell him that Joshua was his, all she had to do was think of Joshua's future. At all costs, her son had to be protected, even if that meant from his own father. Nothing was going to hurt him.

In the end, in all likelihood, Jackson would blow out of both their lives like the wind. Just as he already had once before. Just as he was destined to do again.

A disembodied voice broke into her thoughts, asking, "Yes?"

The nurse. She realized she hadn't removed her finger from the buzzer yet. Mallory pulled it back.

"I'm ready to leave now," she told the woman.

Setting the buzzer and its cord on the center of the bed, Mallory turned around. Jackson's eyes met hers. Holding her son, he made no effort to disguise the fact that he was watching her very intently. That old, weak-kneed feeling threatened to overtake her again and she fought it.

*Into the valley of Death/Rode the six hundred,* Mallory thought.

With any luck, Ursula had already been and gone, leaving everything in its prescribed place. Mallory intended to deal with the clothes nonchalantly as she opened her closet or drawer, making it seem as if they were all just a natural part of her life. She had to make Jackson believe that she was completely involved with Steven. Nothing made a man crazier than wanting something that was unattainable. And he was going to want her, she promised herself. She'd see to it. It would all be perfectly safe, she mused. Jackson wasn't the kind of man to force himself on her if he thought she belonged to someone else.

She slanted a look at him as he turned onto her block. Whatever else he was, Jackson wasn't a lowlife.

Just a jerk.

It occurred to her that Jackson had already been in town for three days. What had he done for a place to sleep in that time? "Where did you stay while I was in the hospital?"

Jackson pulled up into her driveway and pulled up the emergency hand brake. He'd stayed here, but he thought it prudent not to say that just yet. It just seemed easier that way. He'd called his editor, promising to have the book he was working on finished and in on time, then gone shopping. Staying at a hotel hadn't worked into his plans.

"There's a motel right by the hospital," he answered evasively. "Rooms're small, but the view's not all that bad."

She blinked. Then what was the problem? "And the reason you can't stay there now is—?"

He hated hotel rooms. His parents had loved to travel, sometimes taking him with them. True, they'd always gone first class, but the cold, impersonal pristine rooms and expertly made beds turned down by chambermaids he never saw left a feeling of being detached and adrift that he didn't like.

Jackson grinned at her. "Your accommodations are a lot nicer. You're going to need help, remember?" A frown formed on her lips. "And besides, you know I can't work if I'm not comfortable."

Writing didn't come easily to him. He needed to be able to concentrate on his work and nothing else. Hotel rooms always distracted him.

*I think I've had enough of your help already,* she mused, looking into the sleeping face of her son.

She would have wanted to contradict his notion about needing him, but with no siblings and no parents available to stay with her for a little while, she did rather feel alone. No matter how much she resisted, she had to admit that it was nice to have someone staying with her to help out. At least until she slipped into a routine and felt more confident about her abilities.

She supposed that Ursula would have stayed with her in a pinch. But though the older woman was kindhearted, Ursula tended to be a little scatterbrained whenever something akin to an emergency threatened to arise. And midnight feedings and crying babies came under the heading of emergencies.

A lot of things did, Mallory decided, looking at Jackson.

"We'll just see how helpful you turn out to be," she countered.

Jackson was rounding the hood of the car and opening her door before she had a chance to finish what she was saying.

"How's this for starters?" Taking the baby from her, Jackson leaned toward Mallory slightly and offered her the crook of his arm.

Ignoring it, Mallory got out by herself. She felt a little wobblier than she would have liked, like a sailor trying to abandon his sea legs once he came ashore and finding that the process wasn't as easy as he thought.

"Not bad, but I can walk, Jackson."

He wondered what it would take to make her stop being so stubborn. She seemed determined to contradict him every chance she got. "The doctor said not to exert yourself too much at first, remember?"

She led the way up the walk to the front door. "Twenty five steps from bed to bed is not exertion, trust me," she told him over her shoulder. "Besides, I..." Mallory stopped abruptly as Jackson shifted the baby to one side and unlocked the door. Her purse, she realized belatedly, was still in the car, on the floor. Mallory narrowed her eyes. "Where did you get the key?"

He realized his mistake and shrugged carelessly, hoping to cover. "I forgot to get rid of my copy." Forgot, or had been unwilling to, depending on whether or not he believed in Freud and his theory that there was "no such thing as an accident." Jackson pushed the door open and let her enter first. "I, um, found it in the pocket of one of my old jeans."

The rest of his explanation, if there was more, was lost to her as Mallory stared at the profusion of beribboned boxes scattered throughout her living room. On either side of the sofa was an item of baby furniture. On the left stood a swing seat, on the right a beautiful bassinet with a long, flowing skirt.

It was like stumbling into the middle of the baby section in a department store.

Stunned, Mallory looked from the boxes to Jackson, waiting for some plausible explanation. He wasn't offering one. So she asked, "Why did you do this?"

That wasn't exactly what he'd expected to hear. "Because I wanted to." He gently lay the baby in the bassinet. "Um, you had these catalogues in your drawer." He spread his hands wide. He wasn't supposed to be explaining himself. "Some of the things were circled."

This wasn't making any sense. What was he doing going through her desk drawers? "You went back to my office?"

"Yes, to let your boss know that you'd be going on maternity leave. I saw the catalogues earlier, when I was looking for your purse." Jackson's tongue felt thick, heavy. He wasn't supposed to feel as if he'd done something wrong. He was supposed to be fending off her gratitude. "I thought you might want something to look at in the hospital."

It was getting more confused, instead of clearer. Not unlike the lie she'd spun herself. "But you never brought them to me."

He blew out a breath. "I forgot."

She picked up the nearest box on the sofa. Instead of opening it, she turned it around in her hands, weighing it and trying to guess what could possibly be inside. Her eyes never left Jackson.

"You know, for a creative person, you're not doing a very good job of coming up with an explanation for all this."

That's because it was supposed to be understood, not stated. "That's simple. I threw you a shower. The dry kind," he added in case she wanted to take that apart, too.

Box still in hand, Mallory looked at the others piled up on the sofa and the coffee table. He was being too nice. This was really putting a crimp in her plans to get even. "I don't know what to say."

"The words, 'thank you, Jackson', occur to me," he prompted. Jealousy reared its head and had him adding, "If it makes you feel any better, you can tell Steven that you won the lottery."

He was trying to create a schism between her and Steven. That was more like it. She rallied, defending her imaginary relationship. "I don't want to lie to Steven. I don't tell lies, remember?" She wondered if her cheeks were growing hot and if he noticed.

Right about now, it would have given him infinite pleasure to rearrange the errant Steven's face. "All right, when he comes back, I'll tell him you won the lottery."

That meant he intended to remain three weeks. It was absolutely out of the question. Three days would be more like it. There was no way she could hold out against him for three weeks, no matter what her plans. "When he comes back, you won't be here."

Leaning a hip against the sofa, Jackson crossed his arms before him. The more agitated Mallory became, the calmer he grew. They'd always complimented one another like that. "Why, is he the jealous type?"

She intended to give Steven characteristics that were the total antithesis of Jackson's. "No, he's very mild mannered."

Steven was beginning to sound like a first-class wimp. What was the attraction? he wondered. "Then there's no problem."

Her eyes narrowed. "You, Jackson, you're the problem."

Cherubs and newborns shared the expression he wore as he looked at her. "I'm trying not to be."

The hell he wasn't. He was deliberately trying to...what? Make her take him back? That was laughable. He couldn't wait to get away. Why would he want to come back to her now?

She sighed, unable to deal with all this. She felt tired and achy. And then the baby began to fuss.

Jackson saw the glimmer of panic entering her eyes. "Why don't you go change and I'll see if the baby needs to do the same?"

She remained where she was. More surprises. "You know how to change a baby?"

The first night Mallory had to remain at the hospital, Jackson had rented a self-help video on child care and watched it on her VCR. He thought that since he had offered his help, maybe he should learn a little of what was going to be required of him. He really meant to be of use to her. Maybe to make up for the way he'd left so abruptly, maybe to prove to himself that he'd been right to go in the first place. Whatever reason, Jackson always liked to enter a situation well-armed.

He laughed softly and picked up the squirming infant. "You'd be surprised what I know."

He did that so effortlessly. How? When? Were there other children with his face stamped on them that she didn't know about? That would seem likely now, in light of what she was going through.

"Evidently," she murmured.

He watched Mallory as she left the room. The sway of her hips held him prisoner. He'd come back to cure himself of her, but now Jackson was seriously beginning to doubt the wisdom of his return.

# Five

**D**ragging a hand through her tangled hair, Mallory walked into the kitchen. She'd gone through the motions of washing her face, which amounted to throwing a little water at it to try to revive herself.

On a scale of one to ten, she figured right now she measured about a minus two. Mallory was sure she looked like something the cat would have refused to drag in on a dare.

She was going to have to postpone her plans of looking sexy and unattainably alluring until she had more strength available, she decided wearily.

Joshua had been fussing ever since they'd arrived home from the hospital. That was over three hours ago. She'd only just managed to get him to fall asleep. By all rights, she would have dropped in her own tracks right after that, except that hunger pangs were eating away at her with the tenacity of a shrew. She needed to appease them. Dr. Pollack had lectured her at length about how vital good nutrition was since she was breast-feeding. What she ate was instantly recycled into what the baby ate.

No more curling up with a gallon of rocky road and calling it dinner, Mallory thought longingly.

Belatedly, she remembered that there was little else in the refrigerator besides the lightbulb and the shelves. She had intended to go shopping right after work three days ago. The baby's sudden appearance had changed all that.

And left her with an empty refrigerator.

"'She walks in beauty, like the night,'" Jackson quoted, biting his tongue to keep the smile from erupting on his lips.

"Can it, Jackson." The hall mirror had showed her just how bad she looked. She sighed and wished there was a magic wand that could transform her from what would have easily passed as a harpy to that of a presentable woman. "For your information, I'm walking in my sleep." At least it felt that way.

He pushed back from the laptop on the table and studied Mallory for a moment. If exhaustion had a name, it was certainly hers.

"Speaking of sleep, is Joshua finally out?"

Ingrained habit had Mallory opening the refrigerator door even though she knew there was nothing inside it to see.

"Just barely. But I fed and changed him. If I'm very, very good, maybe—" her eyes widened as some of the sleep faded away "—the refrigerator isn't empty."

"The first and second half of your sentence don't agree," Jackson told her absently as he deleted a line. Chewing on his lip, he reversed the order of the words. There, that read better. It might only be a summary, but he was very exacting about what he set down.

She blinked, but everything remained on the shelf just as it had been. Mallory turned to look at Jackson, confused. "Where did all this food come from?"

Damn, what was the word he was looking for? He hated when things just evaporated from his brain like that. "The supermarket."

"You bought all this?"

That wasn't like him, she thought. Jackson wasn't the domestic type. When he had lived here before, he had a housekeeper come in three times a week to do the cleaning and the shopping. She would have been willing to bet that he didn't know a supermarket from a hardware store.

He shrugged, still concentrating on the screen. "I had to. They wouldn't let me steal it." He looked up at her. "I thought you might be hungry. I went shopping yesterday after I left you at the hospital."

Gifts for the baby, roses, food. She would have demanded to know what exactly he thought he was up to if she hadn't been so tired and hungry. But right now, she was thinking with her stomach.

"Incredible," she murmured. Mallory sniffed the air. Something smelled heavenly. "What's that aroma?"

He finished the paragraph before responding. "If your mouth is watering, it's my cologne. If your stomach's reacting, it's probably the lasagna."

Maybe she *had* dropped in her tracks and was sleeping, curled up on the floor in Joshua's room. This *had* to be a dream. "You *made* lasagna?"

He quickly saved his work, pressing two buttons simultaneously before he rose. When he did, he discovered that he was standing much too close to Mallory for either of them to be comfortable. He recovered first.

A wicked grin graced his face. "Will you let me kiss you again if I say yes?"

He was deliberately teasing her. She knew what she looked like. "No."

He took it in stride. There was time. "Then I sent out. There's a great take-out Italian restaurant in the new strip mall not too far from here." He'd found it while riding around last night on his bike. It amazed him how much things had changed. "The area's certainly built up a lot since I was here last."

The area wasn't the only thing that built up, she thought firmly. Her defenses had.

Or so she fervently hoped.

Mallory turned and saw that the microwave was on. He was warming up the food.

Acting as if he'd never left, as if this was his home, Jackson crossed to the cupboard and began rummaging around for the dinnerware. "It was a toss-up between lasagna and pizza." His eyes touched her face gently.

Caressed was more like it, she thought. Instinctively, she took a step backward. As if that would help.

"But I thought we should have something special your first night home," Jackson concluded, taking the plates out.

She could easily get accustomed to this and she knew that would only be a mistake. Because then, when she least expected it, he'd be gone again. This time it would hurt even more than the last time. And the last time had nearly killed her, despite all her bravado to the contrary. She'd never loved a man before. She'd discovered that when she loved, she loved hard. And forever.

*Your plan, remember your plan.* Mallory took the plates from him and set the table herself. "You really didn't have to go through all this trouble."

She was determined not to let him slip back into her life on anything more than a cursory level. He could tell by the set of her chin. There they had a difference of opinion, he mused.

"Yes, my finger's so tired from pushing buttons." His grin almost mocked her. "They delivered while you were busy with Joshua," he added. "I didn't even have to drive to pick it up."

He was twisting things around. He always did have that ability, taking her words and turning them inside out. Mallory frowned. Jackson took down the glasses before she could reach them and set them on the table. "You know what I mean."

"Not usually," he admitted freely. He grew serious. "Look, you're exhausted and if I cooked, the paramedics would have to come by to pay us both a visit. So I called out.

No big deal." He slid a napkin beside each plate. "Learn to accept things graciously."

She didn't take criticism well, even if it was merited. "If I did, I might get accustomed to the things being there." She looked at him pointedly. "And we both know what a mistake that is."

Any trips into the past were going to be strictly to help his cause, not hinder it. Jackson placed a hand on her shoulder and gently pushed her down into a chair. "Sit down, Mallory."

Unable to do otherwise, she sat, turning in her seat to look at him. "Why?"

He took the lasagna tray out of the microwave. "Because eating standing up is tiring."

"You don't have to serve me." But she remained seated, too tired to get up.

Jackson placed the tray on the table, setting a spatula beside it. "All right," he said gamely, "you can serve me."

Not in any manner, shape or form. Those days were over. "In your dreams."

He laughed. "That's what I thought."

Opening the refrigerator, he took out a carton of milk. As he poured the milk into her glass, Mallory made a face. She hated the way milk tasted by itself. She liked her milk hidden in dairy products.

Taking a seat, he cut two symmetrical pieces of lasagna and gave her the first one. "Drink. It's good for the baby."

He was right, but she didn't have to like it. Mallory eyed the glass reluctantly. "Couldn't I just have ice cream and break it down for him that way?"

Jackson grinned, remembering her weakness for ice cream. She'd rather eat ice cream than make love. Almost. "After you finish your dinner," he promised. "If you're good," he added.

Mallory's shoulders instantly straightened. "Good as in how?"

Did she think he was going to pounce on her? She'd just had a baby three days ago, for God's sake. Had he somehow left Mallory with the impression that he was a rutting pig? The thought left an ugly taste in his mouth.

He indicated the dish with his eyes. "As in cleaning your plate."

This just was *not* the Jackson Cain she remembered. The sexy, swaggering writer with the dark soul didn't give a damn about babies, nutrition or postpartum syndrome, the latter of which she was waiting to hit her.

"Jackson, you sound like Mr. Rogers." She sank her fork into the lasagna on her plate and avoided looking into his eyes. "You're beginning to frighten me."

Maybe he was spreading it on a little thick. But she wanted someone upstanding and he was trying his best to measure up. Jackson laid a hand on top of hers. "Would it help if I leered?"

Mechanically, she removed his hand. If she was going to maintain some semblance of sanity, she couldn't let him continue touching her, even in the most innocent fashion. "Help, no, but it would be more in character. I could deal with it."

"All right." He nodded, resuming his meal. If he concentrated on filling his stomach, maybe he wouldn't fill his head with thoughts of her. "Consider yourself leered at."

She laughed to herself. Mallory knew she should be holding him at bay, but it was hard, especially the way she felt at the moment. Later she'd implement her plan. Right now, his attention was awfully flattering.

"Considering that I feel as wide as an airport whose plane has just vacated the hanger, that doesn't sound all that bad."

Jackson shook his head. "You're the smallest looking airport I've ever seen. You don't even look like you were ever pregnant." He saw her expression change. It was a mixture of bemusement and gratitude. And something more he couldn't quite figure out. "What's the matter?" Had he said something wrong?

She frowned, picking at her meal. She'd gone from starving to full in less than five minutes. How was that possible? "You're being nice again."

She'd managed to lose him. "And that's bad?"

Mallory took a deep breath and then slowly blew it out. This was harder than she even imagined when she'd agreed to having him stay over. She didn't need this added ingredient tossed in. She was having a hard enough time trying to hit her stride as a new mother.

"Right now, yes."

He didn't see it that way. Forgetting about the meal, Jackson took her hand in his, enveloping it. He forced her to look at him. "Mallory, just how serious is it between you and Steven?"

She yanked her hand away. Jackson was being a predator again. "How can you ask that?" She looked at him intently. "We just had a baby together."

Mallory purposely worded the statement ambiguously. It was as close as she ever intended to come to telling Jackson the truth. He was part of the 'we' she was referring to.

She knew what he was asking her, Jackson thought, but he put it into words anyway. "I know, but things change between people."

A sadness washed over her. Maybe she should forget about any plans to make him regret what he'd walked out on and just tell him to leave. This was beginning to hurt. "Yes," she said quietly, "I know."

She was talking about them, he thought. But it was far from over between them. He intended to see to that. "Even married people drift apart," he continued persuasively.

Mallory knew what he was trying to do, what she was almost letting him do. Well, she couldn't. There was a small child depending on her to be strong. For his sake, she kept up the charade.

"Steven and I aren't drifting," she insisted.

He wasn't convinced of that. There was no love in her eyes when she said Steven's name. No indication whatsoever that she really cared for the man, baby or no baby. Jackson had seen passion burning there once. Suddenly, he wanted to reclaim that passion. It belonged to him, not to Steven.

"Right," he said sarcastically. He rose and took his plate to the garbage. He'd lost his appetite. "With him in Alaska and you here, you're certainly not floating together."

Mallory tossed her fork down. It landed on the plate with a clatter. "I take it back, you're not being nice. You're just being yourself again." She twisted around to look at him. "If you're going to run Steven down like that, I'm going to have to ask you to leave."

Jackson leaned his back against the sink and looked at her. He didn't need this. He didn't need to feel as if someone had wrenched out his gut and twisted it, tying it into a knot. If he had a grain of sense left, he'd get on his motorcycle and not look back until he arrived in New York.

*Been there. Done that,* a small voice whispered in his mind. *And now look.*

His tone softened, but pride still demanded the words. "Maybe I should."

The baby began to cry again. Jackson saw Mallory wince involuntarily. The argument was temporarily forgotten. She looked exhausted. Delectable, but exhausted.

"In the morning," he amended. With that, he turned and walked out of the kitchen.

She stared at his back. "Where are you going?" she called after him.

"To see if I can still put people to sleep by singing," he said over his shoulder. Jackson stopped in the doorway to smile at her. "It worked with you, once."

She remembered. That was just the problem. She remembered too damn much, she thought. On a whim, he'd taken her to New Orleans for Mardi Gras. They'd partied all night. And then made wild, passionate love in the hotel room. "I'd been up thirty-six hours."

The smile didn't fade one iota. It said he had her number. "That was a hell of a thirty-six hours, wasn't it?"

His words hung in the air after he walked out.

Mallory sighed. This just wasn't going to work. Maybe it *would* be better if he left in the morning. There was no justice. If anyone wound up regretting anything, it was going to be her, not him. Having him around was just going to be sheer torture for her. The sooner he left, the sooner she could work on forgetting him.

*Yeah, right. In a pig's eye.*

So this was what death warmed over felt like, Mallory thought groggily as she stumbled into the kitchen the next morning. Her first night home with Joshua had been nothing short of a trial by fire. Determined to handle it on her own, she'd sent Jackson back to his bed in the guest room and stuck it out through the wee hours of the night, straight into dawn.

Somewhere in there, she'd accumulated five and a half minutes sleep. Maybe six. All she knew was that it wasn't nearly enough to sustain her.

She was even hallucinating, she thought. She was certain she smelled coffee.

She did, she did smell coffee, she thought as the scent grew stronger.

Funny, she didn't remember setting up the coffeemaker timer last night.

That was because she hadn't, she realized, the cobwebs clearing from her eyes. Jackson had. He was sitting here, at the kitchen table, working, a large white mug filled with black liquid beside him.

His computer was open and the opaque screen filled with words she couldn't begin to focus on at this hour in the morning. How did he do it?

"Hi," she mumbled at him, heading straight to the counter with the coffeemaker.

"Hi."

Jackson had been waiting for Mallory to come down ever since he'd gotten up this morning. He'd been tempted to knock on the nursery door, but he'd decided to go along with her wishes and leave her alone. There'd be plenty of opportunities to help out later. The elusive Mitchell wasn't due back for at least another two and a half weeks. That gave him a very large window to work with.

She looked adorable with sleep still heavy on her lids, and her hair rumpled, he thought. The light blue robe was partially open, revealing a shortie nightgown beneath. He fondly remembered her standing like that before him, wearing a robe and nothing more.

Sounding nonchalant took effort when desire licked at him with a hungry tongue. "Rough night?"

Mallory cradled the cup she'd poured as if it contained her very life's blood. Maybe, at this hour of the morning, it did.

"Yes." She took a long, deep sip and let the black liquid work its way through her veins. After a beat she felt almost human again. Almost. Mallory opened her eyes and looked at him. "You seem to have gotten an early start."

He nodded. In lieu of coming to her aid, he'd forced himself to take advantage of the quiet down here and write. "I do my best work in the morning."

She remembered. It never ceased to amaze her how anyone could engage their brain before eight in the morning. Mallory laughed into her cup as she took another sip. "I don't."

He looked up at her then, a smile quirking his lips as he cocked his head. More memories came barging in like insistent storm troopers. "Oh, I don't know. There was that time—"

Alerted, Mallory held up her index finger. "Foul. Rule one."

"Sorry." He laughed, wondering how long he'd have to hold himself in check. He didn't want to, not around her. But if that was what it took to get her back, he'd find a way to manage. "I forgot."

"Apology accepted."

Legs suddenly melting beneath her, she sat down beside him at the table. She wanted to ask him if he'd decided to remain. But asking him would only make Jackson think that she wanted him to. Better to pretend last night's conversation had never taken place and just go from there.

She glanced at the screen. If she concentrated, she could begin to make out letters. "So, what's this one about? Your book," she prompted when he looked at her quizzically.

His work was a very private thing until it took on the shape he was satisfied with. He turned the laptop toward him.

"I'm not sure yet. I'm still finding my way around in it."

She sipped her coffee more slowly, savoring instead of needing. He was here doing research. Or so he said. "You must have some idea what you want to write about."

He did, but he wasn't ready to share it yet. "You know I don't like talking about my plots until after I've written them."

Mallory frowned and continued sipping, chastised. "Sorry."

Her tone alerted him. Jackson looked up. Mallory sounded as if she were withdrawing again. Damn, he realized that he'd just missed a chance to communicate with her. Wasn't that what writing was all about, communicating? That was his stock and trade. Why did he find it so difficult now?

Quickly, Jackson mentally reviewed his notes. "It's a murder mystery set in Newport in the fifties. That's why I had to come back." His eyes touched hers. He was pushing too hard. But eagerness was a new sensation for him. He had to learn how to handle it, let it work for him instead of against him. "To do research."

*And I was hoping it was to see me. Idiot, of course he isn't here to see you.*

Mallory rose abruptly. She was getting carried away. Barriers had to be maintained if this was going to work out the way she wanted.

"Well, don't let me keep you." In the distance, she could hear the tiny wail begin again. With a sigh, Mallory set down her cup. "Looks like I'm being summoned."

Jackson caught her wrist before she could leave. She turned to look at him accusingly. He knew what she was about to say.

"Right, no touching." Jackson dropped her hand immediately. "Nothing personal, I was just trying to stop you from going." A question formed on her lips, but he answered before she could voice it. "Why don't you sit down and have another cup of coffee? It always takes you two to wake up."

Bewilderment creased her brow. He remembered that? "But the baby—"

He was already ahead of her. "I'll see what His Highness wants."

Mallory looked at the computer. He'd stopped in mid-sentence from what she could see. "But you're working." There was nothing Jackson hated more than being interrupted.

Jackson dismissed the protest. "Just some preliminary notes and thoughts, nothing sacred," he assured her. A tolerant smile curved his mouth. "When are you going to stop arguing with everything thing I say?"

She took immediate umbrage. "I'm not arguing, I'm..."

"Arguing," Jackson supplied when her voice trailed off.

Yes, she was arguing. "It's your fault," she accused with what passed as a pout. "You're being too nice. It's throwing me off."

The pout made her look delectable. He resisted the desire to nip her lower lip between his teeth. "Maybe I've just turned over a new leaf."

*And maybe pigs are now jet-propelled.*

* * *

Just as Jackson said, by the time she finished her second cup of coffee, Mallory felt revitalized. She'd also had a chance to peek at the computer screen. Even though all she read was twelve lines, she had to admit that it piqued her interest. Jackson had a way with words that had always captivated her, pulling her right into the story from the very first line. She'd read all his books.

And trashed a few, Mallory recalled ruefully. It had been childish, but it had made her feel better at the time.

And what was going to make her feel better after he left her this time?

She bit her lip, working it slowly as she thought. Why had he returned? With information being as abundant and available as it was these days, he could get what he needed from a database. What he'd given her had been just a flimsy excuse. There had to be another reason why he'd returned.

What was it?

A noise caught her attention, pulling her back into the kitchen. Jackson entered, holding Joshua. She couldn't help thinking how natural he looked with the baby tucked against his side. Who would have ever thought it? Certainly not her. She would have bet any amount of money that he was the type to run the other way as soon as the first tiny wail was heard.

Jackson held the baby up, turning him in Mallory's direction. "See, here she is, Josh. She hasn't abandoned you. Mom's just taking a breather."

It felt as if she'd been dropped bodily into a greeting card ad. What made it so implausible was that she was in it with Jackson, the original rebel. Any minute now, she was going to wake up. At the very least, the other shoe would drop. Undoubtedly on her foot.

Smiling, she pushed back her chair. "Hi, sweetie. What's he been telling you, hmm?"

Jackson grinned as he brought the baby to her. "Nothing but the best. Seems he's hungry and I can't begin to accommodate him there. Unless you want to start him on formula.''

Not yet. That would come later, when she went back to work. It would make life simpler. Right now, she just wanted to enjoy bonding with him.

Mallory looked at Jackson as she took the baby from him. ''How do you know he's hungry?''

How could such a tiny thing have such a choke hold on his heart so quickly? he wondered. It didn't seem possible. And yet it was. ''When he started sucking on my knuckle, I figured it was a sign.''

Moving behind her, Jackson laid a hand on Mallory's shoulder as he looked down at the baby in her arms. A sweet longing went through him. A longing accompanied by an upbraiding. If he hadn't left, this family could have been his instead of some other man's.

It still could, he told himself. Mallory had been his before she'd been Steven's.

Steven. That reminded him. He'd prowled around the house earlier, when she'd been in the hospital, trying to discover what his competition looked like. Jackson still didn't have a clue.

He asked now. ''What does he look like?''

Yes, he was hungry, she thought, watching as the baby's mouth was rooting around her finger. ''Who?''

''Steven.'' She turned to look at Jackson quizzically. He went on, wondering about the strange look that had entered her eyes. ''I noticed you didn't have any photographs of him anywhere. Why?''

*Oh, damn.* ''He doesn't like having his photograph taken.''

No one minded being captured on film more than he did and she'd still managed to get a few photographs of him while they'd been together. Something didn't sound quite right.

''Why? Is he ugly?''

Mallory stepped back, still facing him, wanting distance between them.

"No, he's not ugly," she snapped defensively. "He's—" What? Shy? What could she use as an excuse and still have it sound plausible?

"Amish?" Jackson supplied glibly when her voice trailed off.

"Yes." Without thinking, Mallory leaped at the excuse, then realized that Jackson was being flippant. "I mean, no, he's not. At least, not anymore." She was tripping over her own tongue. "He was." Did that sound lame, or what? Why couldn't she think straight around him? "But old habits are hard to break." Turning the tables, Mallory looked at him pointedly. "You should know that."

"Point taken," Jackson conceded with a nod. "Still, it does seem rather odd that you wouldn't have a photograph of him *somewhere.*"

"I do," Mallory countered with feeling. She touched her heart. "Right here. Now if you'll excuse me, I have a hungry little man to see to. Thanks for the coffee." Her voice was cool, distant, just as she wished she could be. "You still make the best around."

"Nice to hear." Jackson looked after her thoughtfully. All the pieces definitely weren't fitting together.

# Six

This just wasn't working.

Oh, it worked on a superficial level. Mallory hummed under her breath to soothe Joshua as she shifted him to her other breast. Jackson had said he would help her take care of the baby and she couldn't fault him for his efforts.

As a matter of fact, he'd turned out to be far better at it than she would have ever guessed. Whenever he was around Joshua, Jackson displayed infinite patience and his very presence seemed to comfort and tranquilize the baby. As a matter of fact, Joshua hardly ever fussed when Jackson was around him. Helping with the baby was one of those things Jackson took to effortlessly. But then, she'd always known that he had a gift for being able to do whatever he set his mind to.

If Mallory thought he'd soon tire of helping her, Jackson certainly didn't show any signs of it. It had been over a week and a half since he'd reappeared in her life, hers and Joshua's and, if anything, he was getting better at the little

jobs that went into tending for an infant, not worse. He
helped bathe the baby and took his turn at diapering and
walking the floor. He never complained that the baby kept
him up, or interfered with his oh-so-fragile working schedule.

This was a side of himself that Jackson had never displayed before, an aspect of him she hadn't dreamed existed.

No, the problem didn't lay with Jackson keeping his
word, it lay with him keeping it all too well. Lulling her into
a comfortable state from which she knew only a rude awakening would expel her.

And the rude awakening was coming. Just as sure as the
sun rose every morning.

In the meantime, she was becoming far too accustomed
to Jackson just being there every day. Though she tried to
fight it, Mallory was becoming used to waking up each
morning to the aroma of strong coffee wafting into her
room. Strong coffee that was somehow mingled in with the
scent of his cologne. It seemed to pervade every corner of
the house, seeking her out whenever she thought to hide
from it. And from him.

Like air, there was no escaping Jackson's influence in her
life. As for her plan to make him suffer for leaving her, that
had somehow been lost in the shuffle of daily living as she
tried to get her bearings in this new world she'd found herself in.

Joshua whimpered again. It was a frustrated sound that
echoed with Mallory. With a helpless sigh, she shifted
Joshua back to the right side. His rooting mouth did the
rest.

Maybe it would work better this time, she hoped. Mallory looked down at the tiny, puckered face at her breast.

She blinked back tears. Everything felt as if it were going
awry.

Unsatisfied, hungry, Joshua whimpered, this time more
loudly. The muffled sound rippled against her skin, send-

ing minor shock waves of guilt through her. Her frown was deep, cutting right down to the bone. She felt tears of disappointment gathering in her eyes.

Damn it, what was wrong with her? For the first few days, it seemed as if she could have fed two babies and had enough left over for a third. Now, suddenly, for no apparent reason, she couldn't even produce enough to satisfy Joshua. She was drying up and she didn't know why.

Mallory pressed her lips together. Crying wasn't going to help the situation. It wouldn't change anything. It never did.

"Try a little harder, honey," she coaxed softly, stroking the baby's downy head. "Maybe Mommy just needs to be kick started."

"I never heard it called that before."

Starting, her head jerked up as Mallory looked toward the doorway. Jackson was standing there, a strange expression on his face. He was grinning, and yet, it was as if the grin were masking something more. Something she couldn't begin to read.

It didn't change the fact that he had no business standing there, ogling her at a time like this. Her eyes narrowed in silent accusation. Shifting on the rocking chair so that her back was to him, she asked, "What are you doing here?"

"I knocked," he explained, "but you didn't answer."

He'd pushed the door open slowly and then been totally captivated by what he saw. He'd seen her completely nude, much less seminude, more times than he could count, but there was something almost poetic about the way she looked when he'd walked in.

He wanted to drink in the sight, save it the way he saved everything, to be reprocessed onto the pages of his books. Every word he wrote was propelled by emotions, by feelings that he kept in a repository until he needed them. He only made withdrawals when he was writing.

Until Mallory.

Without speaking, without asking, she demanded more of him than he had ever given anyone else. He had to be truer to her, be more honest. Worse than that, he wanted to be. And so, he had run, afraid of the intensity of what he felt, afraid of being depleted beyond hope of ever recapturing what he had lost. Afraid that it would forever rob him of his creative edge.

Looking at her now, he didn't understand how he'd ever had the strength to leave.

Jackson cleared his throat, wishing his mind was as easy to vacate. "I was just going to make a quick run to the store and wanted to know if you needed anything."

Mallory raised her eyes to the reflection in the window. She saw herself captured in it, a transparent image with her hair about her shoulders and a baby at her breast. And he was looking at her.

A tinge of embarrassment mixed with pleasure and brought color to her cheeks. "You're staring."

He was and he couldn't help it. "Sorry." Shoving his hands into his pockets, he looked at something harmless. The changing table he had helped her assemble. It seemed an odd thing to apologize for, being mesmerized by a beautiful, natural sight.

She shifted, uncomfortable with the gaze in his eyes. And drawn to it at the same time. Holding the baby against her shoulder, she covered herself quickly, slipping the blouse back into place.

Only then did she turn to face him. "It's not like you haven't seen it before."

He surprised her by shaking his head. "Never quite that way." The words were soft, whispered so that they glided along her skin. The sight of Mallory with a baby at her breast was something that would always remain burned into the recesses of his mind.

She patted Joshua's back, rubbing it in small, concentric circles. *I'm sorry, Baby. So sorry.*

"Why aren't you working?" She half expected Jackson to say something flippant about her affecting his concentration. It wouldn't be the first time.

Crossing to her, he couldn't resist tickling the tiny foot that was sticking out from underneath the baby's sack. He watched Joshua's face as, distracted, the baby wrinkled his nose and made a sound very close to a giggle.

Why did that make him feel as if sunshine were bursting in his veins?

"I'm done for the morning," Jackson told her after a beat.

When she'd passed by the kitchen earlier on her way upstairs, Mallory had seen Jackson hunched over his computer, so deep in thought that he hadn't even heard her go by. He'd always claimed that writing was both agony and ecstasy for him. And more the former than the latter.

"So soon?"

Jackson glanced at her before looking at the baby again. Joshua was trying to consume Mallory's blouse, starting with the shoulder pad. Gently, he extracted the material from the baby's mouth.

"Amazing, isn't it?" he commented.

Actually, he mused, it was. It normally took him a long time to work things through. Words didn't come pouring out of him the way they did from some other writers. Each paragraph, each line, each word emerged on the screen only after a torturous process. It had to be just right before it joined its brethren. That took a great deal of time and a great deal out of him.

This time however, he'd all but breezed through the set amount of writing he had scheduled for himself. It was still time-consuming by other standards, but by his own, he was writing like a house afire. He hadn't expected it to come to him this easily.

It had to be her influence, which made the situation rather ironic. It had been fear of her influence that had made him leave in the first place.

Maybe, he mused thoughtfully, looking at Mallory, it was time he reexamined things.

Mallory moved away from him and toward the window. Trying to escape him, he thought. For the time being, he remained where he was.

"Anyway, I thought I'd get something to eat for tonight and I wanted your input." Jackson pushed the rocking chair with the tip of his finger. It swayed gently. "You're upset," he observed.

Though his writing might be going great guns, other, even more important things were not faring nearly as well. Progress with Mallory was slow even compared to the flow of molasses in January.

He read her expression the only way he could. Jackson nodded toward the doorway. "Want me to leave?"

*Yes, stop messing with my life, Jackson. I'm not some heroine leaping out of your word processor. Things won't clear up within x number of pages.*

That wasn't fair, she thought. If there was anything she was, it was fair. He might not be, but that didn't alter things for her. She wasn't the type to indulge in revenge.

Biting her lower lip, Mallory shook her head. "No, it's not you. It's just that..." Her voice trailed off, sinking into helplessness.

Joshua filled in the silence, whimpering again. The whimper turned into a full-fledged wail.

Jackson's attention changed direction instantly. He approached her, not heeding the warning in her eyes. "Something wrong with the baby?" He looked at Joshua. The baby looked no different than he had this morning when he'd come into the nursery in response to an indignant wail which Jackson had ultimately translated into: Change me.

Mallory shook her head so hard, her hair bounced on her shoulders. "No, with me."

Gently, Jackson took the baby from her and began to rock him. Settling down, Joshua curled up against his shoulder.

"What?" When Mallory made no response, Jackson placed a hand on her shoulder, silently urging her on. She raised her eyes to his and he saw misery there. Was he responsible for that?

"Mallory, you like to talk more than any person I know." They were complete opposites in that. His medium had been pen and paper. Hers had been life itself. It had been one of the things that had drawn him to her in the first place. "You always wanted to talk things through." He'd been the one who had been reticent, preferring to leave things unsaid. If you didn't say words, you didn't have to bother taking them back later.

Restless, she moved away from him again. And their son, she thought.

God, why did it ache so much to see them together like that? To know she couldn't risk telling him and wanting to.

*Bad move,* she told herself. *Very bad move.*

Mallory lifted her shoulder and let it drop. "Well, maybe I've changed."

He sincerely doubted that would ever happen. If it did, it would be everyone's loss. "Not that much. That would be tantamount to a snow leopard suddenly turning a bright pink."

The baby had fallen asleep, lulled by the sound of Jackson's voice rumbling out of his chest, vibrating against his cheek. Very gently, Jackson eased the baby down into the crib. Covering the small form, he backed away from the crib. He took Mallory's hand and slipped out of the room.

"Out with it," he ordered. "Maybe I can help."

Mallory closed the door, leaving it open a crack. She laughed softly to herself as she walked down the stairs. Jackson was right behind her. "Since when did you think you could fix everything?"

"Not everything," he corrected, following her down the stairs. "Just some things. You never know until you try."

Determined to maintain her silence on the subject, Mallory didn't bother answering. Reaching the landing, he caught her by the wrist, turning her around. She was surprised by the intense look on his face. For a moment, if she let herself, she could almost believe that he did care. That it mattered to him how she felt.

But that would only be deluding herself in the long run. Men who cared didn't bail out.

"Look, being this bright and chipper isn't easy for someone who was born brooding, Mallory. But I am trying."

Undecided, tempted, she searched his face for a clue. This wasn't just lip service he was paying. For whatever reason, he *did* care. At least for the moment.

"Yes," she agreed, "you are trying." She blew out a breath as she looked up at the ceiling. God, but she felt inadequate. "I'm drying up."

He didn't quite understand her meaning. "That used to be my line."

How well she knew that. Impatience, with him, with herself, deepened her frown. "Not creatively. Physically."

It pained her to admit anything so intimate to him. She wanted to keep him locked out of her life on all levels.

*Then you should have never let him stay.*

He still looked as if he didn't quite comprehend. "Joshua's hungry and I can't feed him, okay?"

"Oh—" He thought of the formula that the nurse had given Mallory just as they'd left the hospital. Obviously a lot of mothers chose that route. He didn't see the big deal.

"Yes, 'oh.'" Mallory threw up her hands and walked away. She talked too much, she thought reprovingly. He had no business knowing that. It wasn't as if he could help or anything.

He followed her into the kitchen, unwilling to be shut out this way. She was obviously suffering. "Maybe it's just temporary."

That didn't help the situation now. She turned on him. "Meanwhile, how does he eat?"

This wasn't just about being dry, he thought. This was about a lot of things. He bore the brunt of her anger because he knew that he deserved it. He owed it to her to let her work some of it through. Maybe when she did, they'd have a chance together. If he found a way to get Steven out of the picture.

"Formula," he suggested. "Call your doctor, call his pediatrician. Call the nurses' hotline." A half-dozen possible solutions came to mind. "Talk to someone who can make you feel better about this."

He did care, she thought again. For whatever reason, maybe because he was bonding with the baby on his own level, or because some part of him felt guilty, he cared.

"I already am." She just hadn't realized it before. Before he could say anything else and ruin it, she smiled at him. "Thanks." She tried to think. It wasn't always easy, this close to him. "They did give me some formula for him," she recalled.

She opened the pantry's double doors and began to scavenge through the bottom shelf. Where had she put it? "I kept it, just in case."

Jackson crouched down beside her. She looked at him quizzically as he pushed aside a box of cake mix. "You've gotten more practical since..." He didn't want to say since the last time he'd been with her. There was no sense in emphasizing that. "Well, since." He let it drop there.

There it was, she thought. Behind the unopened box of oatmeal. The oatmeal she meant to throw out the next time she succumbed to a bout of spring cleaning fever. Mallory reached in and pulled out the small, complimentary six-pack of formula.

She glanced over her shoulder. Had Jackson just given her a compliment, or a dig? "And you've gotten more thoughtful."

Rising, he helped her to her feet. His mouth quirked. "I was always thoughtful."

Too close, he was too close. Mallory turned away. "Sorry, I must have been thinking of my other lover."

His jaw tightened ever so slightly at the thought of the other man. She caught the change out of the corner of her eye.

"Were you?" he asked.

She huffed, annoyed. Opening the cupboard beside the sink, she took out a small bottle with a dancing pink elephant on it. The elephant was wearing gleaming white diapers. The bottle was a gag gift she'd gotten at the baby shower Ursula had thrown for her.

"It was a joke, Jackson."

He pulled off one of the cans of formula from the plastic retainer that held it cleaved to its brethren and offered it to her.

"Speaking of jokes," he said glibly, "didn't Steven make any arrangements to call you at all while he was away?"

*Here we go again.* This lie was threatening to completely engulf her. She felt like Pinocchio after his nose had begun sprouting.

"Of course he did." She yanked open the kitchen drawer, looking for a can opener. She pulled it so hard, the drawer came off the runner. Silverware rained down on the patterned vinyl floor. "Now look what you've done," she snapped.

"Me? You're the one whose hand is on the drawer," he said, pointing out needlessly. Squatting down, he scooped up the various utensils and tossed them back into the drawer.

"Not like that," she chastised. "They have to be washed."

"Why?" He looked down at the silverware. "The floor's clean."

Mallory just rolled her eyes. Taking the filled drawer from him, she dumped the contents into the sink.

Making himself useful, Jackson poured formula into the bottle while Mallory quickly rinsed off the fallen silverware.

"So?" The single word stretched out, asking for an answer.

She knew he wasn't going to give up until she gave it to him. He was asking about Steven. Well, she'd started it. She had no one to blame but herself.

Mallory tossed wet silverware onto the dish rack. "So, there wasn't supposed to be another phone call for another week." Mind scrambling like a goat over slippery mountain peaks, she threw together a story, improvising as she went. "He already called me when he reached the airport in Alaska. What he said was that he'd try to get a call patched through in a couple of weeks or so."

She could see that her spurt of creativity was wasted. Jackson didn't look as if he was buying this. That was his problem. She intended to stick to this with her dying breath.

Mallory threw the last fork onto the rack, turning to face him squarely. "Look, he has a lot on his mind. It isn't easy being a civil engineer."

A brow rose. "I thought you said he was a petroleum engineer."

Damn, she had. "I did," she covered. "He's both. He had a split major in college." The story was getting away from her, but she refused to surrender. She could still make this work. "This way he'd cover all his bets."

Jackson took a towel and began wiping the utensils. "He must have been very tired, doing all that studying." He dropped several spoons into the drawer.

"Yes, he was." She held up her head, daring Jackson to contradict her. "Steven held down a full-time job and went to school at night. It took him longer." She took out a saucepan and filled it with water, then shifted the pan onto a burner on the stove. With the flame on low, she placed the bottle into it. "That's why his career is so important to him."

"I see." He nodded slowly, as if assimilating the information. It was hard to keep from grinning. "That would probably explain why he's so stiff."

She turned to look at him. "Stiff? What are you talking about?"

Several more pieces of silverware joined the others, rattling against the ones that were already in the drawer. "His underwear still has creases in it, as if the cardboard had just been removed."

She'd intended for Jackson to just glance at the neat pile, not take any of them out to examine. "You went rummaging through Steven's underwear?" she demanded heatedly.

Jackson's expression was the last word in innocence. "Nothing kinky, Mallory. I was looking for something." Proof that the man didn't spend the night here the way she claimed. It would have been a small consolation, but he'd take what he could get.

Guilt hopscotched through her. It was a day for guilt, she thought ruefully. But in this case it wasn't merited. She didn't owe Jackson an explanation *or* the truth.

"Did you find it?" she asked coldly.

"Not really. So tell me," he said as he retired the dish towel on the rack, "is there a reason why his underwear is so unused looking?"

Her eyes narrowed to slits. He was baiting her, she thought. She'd die before admitting the lie. She intended to go down fighting. "They're ironed." Jackson's brow rose higher. She could have punched him. "He's very fastidious about his things. He likes everything to be neat and tidy."

Jackson nodded, as if he was taking the explanation in stride. "Very commendable."

He was patronizing her, the louse. "You make it sound as if you don't believe me."

"It's not that, exactly." His eyes searched hers, looking for the truth. A truth he could live with, not necessarily the real one. "I can't think of a reason why you'd lie about having a lover."

Indignation flared in her eyes, turning them a bright green. "That's because I'm not lying. Look, he's away, but he'll be back. I'm here." She turned off the burner. "His son's here. His clothes are here."

"Very true."

On impulse, Mallory took his hand and dragged him back up the stairs to her bedroom. "C'mere." With a flourish, she threw open the closet door and pulled out a shirt sleeve. "See?"

"Nice taste," Jackson commented placidly. He took the hanger out. "I see stiffness isn't an exclusive property of just his underwear." He pretended to examine the shirt. "There're are creases in his shirt as well."

She yanked the hanger from his hand. She'd had just about enough of his snide remarks. "They were just freshly laundered, that's all. I ironed them, too," she added proudly. Though he'd made love to her almost every day, Jackson had never mentioned moving in with her, even though she had secretly hoped that he would. She wanted him to envy the relationship she had with Steven.

God, she was beginning to act as if the man were real, she thought. Her head started to ache.

Jackson's eyes traveled over the shirt. "Tell me, is Steven a masochist or doesn't he feel them?"

"Them?" She stared at Jackson. "What are you talking about? What 'them?'"

"Pins, Mallory." He took one out of the shirt and held it up for her to examine. "There are pins stuck in the collar and the front of the shirt." He handed it to her. "I can't see how Steven would put on his shirts without scarring himself for life." Jackson allowed his expression to soften to just a hint of a smile. "That is, if this former Amish man of yours is normal."

Damn it, why hadn't Ursula been more careful? For that matter, why hadn't she? She should have taken a closer look at the shirts. But all she'd wanted was for him to see them hanging there, nothing more.

"And they're, what?" He looked inside the collar. "Size 18." He shifted the shirts to one side and took out a pair of slacks. "But I see that he wears 32 long pants. Near as I can figure it, you're in love with a man who's built like a Q-Tip.

Long and lanky, with all the girth on top. Does he have trouble staying on his feet during the Santa Ana winds?''

Stumped for a way out, she went on the defensive. ''If you're going to be sarcastic, I'm not going to dignify your questions with an answer.''

Pulling the hanger out of his hands, she jammed it back in the closet and walked out.

Mallory realized that she'd left the bottle standing downstairs and she could hear Joshua beginning to fuss again. She went down the stairs quickly.

Jackson hurried behind her. ''I'm not being sarcastic, Mallory.''

She threw him an exasperated look over her shoulder. ''No?''

''All right, I'm being sarcastic,'' he conceded, walking into the kitchen after her. ''But maybe that's because I'm annoyed.''

She tested the formula against her wrist. Perfect. ''You have no right to be annoyed with me.'' Her eyes met his. Hers were bright with anger. ''You walked out on me, remember?''

He remembered. He remembered all too vividly. ''I'm not annoyed with you. I'm annoyed with me *because* I walked out on you.'' He paused, looking for a way to force the words from his mouth. Admitting this wasn't easy for him. ''Maybe I went too quickly.''

''Maybe,'' she conceded, some of the heat leaving her words.

For a moment, she vacillated, wanting desperately to tell him that Joshua was his son, knowing that if she did, she'd regret it. Better that she had her pride intact. In the end, that would be all she'd have left. That, and Joshua of course.

She looked down at the bottle in her hand. It was like an anchor, grounding her to reality. ''Um, the baby's still hungry.''

He nodded. "You'd better go and feed him." He remembered the original reason he'd sought her out in the nursery. "Anything you want at the store?"

*Yes, a brand new start.* She nodded, taking down the pad and pencils housed in a magnetic holder which rested on the side of the refrigerator. "Give me a minute, I'll make a quick list."

By the time Jackson returned, she'd fed Joshua. He'd consumed the formula greedily and then dozed off, leaving her with a bittersweet feeling. She was glad his hunger was sated, but saddened that she'd failed him.

She'd come downstairs just as Jackson entered through the back door. He had four plastic bags suspended from each wrist.

"They're groceries, Jackson, not weights. Why are you carrying all of them in at the same time?"

It hadn't occurred to him to do it any other way. He also hadn't meant to buy so much, but one item after another had found its way into the cart.

"I hate making unnecessary trips." With a thud, he deposited all eight bags onto the table and then disentangled his wrists from the plastic hoops.

"Beats getting a hernia."

Mallory began unpacking the first bag. Taking out a box, she read the label. She didn't remember asking for the sugary cereal. Mallory raised a brow in Jackson's direction and he merely smiled. How could a man with such a gorgeous body maintain it by putting such junk food into it?

His gorgeous body, she reminded herself, was no longer any business of hers.

"Oh, by the way," she said nonchalantly, "guess what? Steven called."

"While I was out." How convenient, Jackson mused. He took a half gallon container of milk and placed it on the bottom shelf in the refrigerator.

She didn't care for his tone. "He wasn't calling you, he was calling me."

He took out a bag of potatoes and placed it on the counter. "So what did he have to say?"

She kept her back to Jackson. It was easier spinning lies when she didn't have to look at his face. "He was excited about his son, of course. And sorry he wasn't here to be with me."

He stopped unpacking and looked at her. "Did you tell him about me?"

Her mouth was growing dry. It took effort to sound cheerful. "Yes, I did." She stacked several six-packs of the formula in the pantry. "He's very grateful to you for being there in his place."

Grateful. That would hardly be the word he'd use. "Better man than I," Jackson conceded. He started emptying another bag. "If Steven had been here in my place, I'd want to rip out his liver."

She glanced at him. Humor curved her mouth. "I see you haven't lost any of your mild mannered, diplomatic verve."

He lifted a shoulder carelessly. "Not so's you'd notice." His eyes met hers over the oranges. "You can be diplomatic about a lot of things, Mallory, but a man's woman, well, I think that goes beyond the boundaries of diplomacy, wouldn't you?"

She wasn't going to let him bait her. And she wasn't going to remember, either. Not about wanting to be his, not anything about them.

"Well, fortunately, Steven isn't like that. He's very levelheaded and calm. Without a jealous bone in his body," she added.

Jackson snorted at the image. In his book, that wasn't an attribute, that was the absence of feeling. "Vanilla ice cream."

She turned around, looking at the kitchen table and the remaining bags. "Where?"

He placed himself between her and the table, blocking her view. Forcing Mallory to look at only him.

"Not where, who. This Steven of yours sounds like vanilla ice cream. Good in a pinch, but not very satisfying overall."

"He's not vanilla ice cream and he's very satisfying," she insisted heatedly.

Jackson let a bag slip from his hands. Apples tumbled onto the floor, scattering like huge red marbles. He ignored them. He didn't know whether or not to believe that Steven existed. Half of him doubted it, the other half thought those doubts were wishful thinking. He grabbed her by the shoulders as she began to stoop down to pick up the apples.

"Is he, Mallory?" he demanded, jealousy rubbing callused hands over him.

She lifted her chin defiantly. "Yes."

Mallory couldn't have hurt him any more than if she had tried.

"Does he satisfy you like this?"

Without thinking, going only on instinct, Jackson bracketed her shoulders between his hands and brought his mouth down to hers. He had no intentions of being gentle. Nor did he have intentions of being swept away, either. Jackson only meant to remind her of what they'd once had. It wasn't supposed to remind him as well. But it did. Oh, so vividly.

Her mouth felt like satin.

Jackson pulled her closer to him, his arms tightening around her, his mouth slanting over hers, crushing hers. He could feel Mallory's heart pounding against his chest. Or was that *his* heart racing that way? He wasn't sure. Wasn't sure of anything except that a man could barely survive lightning striking him the way it was right now.

Lightning, pure lightning, that's what she was. Who was teaching who?

Mallory moaned, held helplessly in the grip of the passion that instantly erupted when he kissed her. Nothing had changed. She was its prisoner.

And his.

Desire battered her body, begging for release. And all she could do was beg for mercy.

Stop, he had to stop, Jackson thought desperately. Before he couldn't.

# Seven

There was absolutely no breath left in her lungs. No breath available in her entire body. It had all been sucked out, taken away by the force of his kiss. And either the room was suddenly tilting, or her head was spinning. Badly.

She had to struggle to form words and push them out. "This wasn't a contest, Jackson. You don't get to collect the marbles again."

Mustering what tiny shred of dignity she could find, Mallory walked out of the room on legs that felt as if they belonged to someone else. She wasn't quite sure how she made it, but she managed to reach the living room before collapsing.

Knees giving way, she sank onto the sofa like a rag doll.

*Oh boy,* she thought, running her hand along her mouth. She could feel her lips vibrating with his imprint. *Oh boy, oh boy, oh boy.*

She'd left him speechless. Utterly speechless and numb. At least, the parts that hadn't ignited. If he'd begun to entertain the idea that Mallory didn't love Steven before, he was convinced of it now. Angry, hurt, he'd kissed her to prove a point. That she still cared a little.

He'd proven it all right. And then some. He'd proven to her and to himself as well that she cared more than a little.

And so did he.

But that didn't give him the right to force himself on her. And that was ultimately what he'd done. She hadn't wanted to kiss him. Not at the outset. The next time, and there would be a next time he promised himself, it was going to have to be her lead, not his. There was no other way to convince her that they belonged together.

He walked into the living room and saw her sitting on the sofa, her shoulders hunched as if against the cold. Guilt and longing exchanged dance cards.

"Mallory," he said quietly. She raised her head, but didn't turn around to look at him. He talked to the back of her head. It was easier that way. "I'm sorry."

"Yes," she said quietly. "Me, too." *More than you'll ever know.*

Shaken, contrite, Jackson withdrew from the room.

"No, there's nothing wrong with you. You seem to have bounced back magnificently, just like your friends. I appear to be having a bumper crop this season, all of you fit and ready to return to a normal life within two weeks of delivery."

Dr. Sheila Pollack smiled at Mallory as she slowly rose from the small stool beside the stirrups on the examining table. The smile was a little stiff around the edges, but it had nothing to do with Mallory or her recovery. It had to do with her.

Sheila despised this clumsy feeling that was taking hold of her. Agile, athletic, she had managed to come this far along in her pregnancy without slowing down. But it was finally catching up to her. And she absolutely hated it.

Now she felt as unwieldy as a house. The long, flowing lab coat she favored, the one that had done such an excellent job of hiding her ever widening waist all these months, no longer closed at all. The two ends hung on either side of her protruding belly like two tall, thin columns, emphasizing her girth with their slender appearance.

Mallory sat up, clutching the yellow-and-white striped sheet to her. The examining room was cold by design and she shivered. It didn't make sense. If she was all right, then why was she having difficulties?

"But then why aren't I producing milk anymore?"

Sheila shrugged and shook her head. "Sometimes, these things happen. Women go dry. That was one of the reasons they had wet nurses in the old days." Stripping off her plastic gloves, Sheila stepped on the metal pedal attached to the small waste basket. The lid yawned open and she tossed the gloves inside. "That, and convenience, of course. A lot of things could be the cause."

Sheila took a dab of hand lotion from the dispenser beside the tissues on the counter and rubbed it vigorously over her hands. She enumerated just two. "Hormones ping-ponging within our bodies, trying to level out after the birth process. Tension."

Sheila looked at Mallory closely. They had developed more than a doctor-patient bond, though the latter went back over several years. Mallory had also sold Sheila the condo she was presently living in. Over the course of time, they'd gotten together socially on several occasions. Though only a few years separated them, Sheila had maternal feelings toward the younger woman. Beneath the feisty independence that the world saw was a vulnerable woman.

Not, Sheila mused, unlike herself.

She guessed at the source of Mallory's agitation. "It doesn't make you any less of a mother, Mallory."

Mallory bit her lip, still feeling frustrated and helpless. "I know, but . . . I feel like I've failed him somehow."

"Don't." Sheila laid a comforting hand on her shoulder. "You can still hold him, love him, be there for him."

She smiled warmly. There was no doubt in her mind that Mallory would make an excellent mother. Those who cared always did. Sheila thought of her own parents, wealthy in everything but emotions. There were far more important things than just providing for physical needs.

"Just because his food container has changed doesn't mean anything else has." Sheila made a few perfunctory notes on Mallory's chart. There was no need to see her again until her annual exam. "Love is always the most important ingredient."

Mallory thought of Jackson and of what she couldn't have. "Yes, I know."

The sadness in her tone alerted Sheila. She laid down her pen and looked at Mallory.

"Is there anything else on your mind? Anything you want to talk about?" She closed the chart and tucked it under her arm. "My schedule's full this morning, but we could meet after five for some tea." She knew Mallory favored Earl Grey. "Barring a sudden baby's appearance, of course," she added with a smile.

These days, that was beginning to include herself in the group as well. She'd been an obstetrician long enough to be prepared for any contingencies. Babies didn't always adhere to calendars. Hers was due toward the end of April and everything looked as if it was going according to schedule, but she knew better than to dismiss an early birth.

Mallory shook her head. This wasn't anything that anyone could help her with. This was something she was going to have to work through herself. She wiggled her way off the table, still keeping the sheet tucked around her.

"No, I'm fine. Really."

Sheila had never been one to press. "Well, I'm here if you change your mind." She gave Mallory's arm a little squeeze and felt the tension residing there. "Things have a way of working themselves out. Just relax and everything'll be all right.''

Mallory nodded. That was just it. She couldn't relax. Not really. Not as long as Jackson remained anywhere near her.

Not when she was waiting for him to leave again.

*Once burned...* she thought with resignation, hurrying into her clothes.

The important issue here, she reminded herself as Sheila closed the door behind her, leaving her to get dressed, was her son. She was relieved that she wasn't failing him as a mother, even if she was letting tension rob Joshua of his rightful food.

She made it a point to stock up on formula before she returned home. The six-packs Jackson had bought at the store a few days ago were almost gone.

He was on his feet as soon as he heard her key in the lock, dropping his newspaper to the sofa. His mind hadn't really been on it anyway. He'd read the same paragraph a half-dozen times without absorbing it. Normally, preoccupation bothered him, but his writing had gone so well early this morning that nothing was going to faze him.

Unless it had to do with Mallory. She'd left for her two-week exam convinced that there was something physically inadequate with her. He could have told her that there wasn't, but she needed to hear it from her doctor in order to believe it.

At least he hoped that was what she heard from her doctor.

"So, what did the doctor say?"

Mallory jumped as Jackson closed the door behind her. She hadn't expected him to be right there.

"The doctor said I can go back to work if I want to." She stepped out of her shoes, leaving her purse on the table beneath the mirror as she walked into the living room.

He took the bag of formula from her, going to the kitchen with it. That hadn't been what he'd meant. But since she'd phrased it that way, his curiosity had been aroused.

"And do you want to?"

Tired, still wound up, she sank down onto the sofa and put her feet up on the coffee table. "It's not a matter of wanting to. I have to earn a living." It helped, though, she added mentally, that she really loved her job, and could keep Joshua with her some of the time.

Closing the pantry, Jackson reentered the living room. He crossed to the sofa and looked down at her. At any angle, she was beautiful. His heart ached just to look at her.

"What about Steven?" Despite his best intentions, a touch of mockery escaped, tingeing his words. "What about his obligation?"

That was easy. She told Jackson the reason she had never gotten in contact with him to let him know that he was going to be a father. "I don't want him to feel obligated to pay for anything."

Jackson took the words at face value. Leaning back on the sofa, he crossed his arms and studied her expression. "Sounds like there's trouble in paradise."

She wasn't so tired that she couldn't get angry. She swung her legs down from the table. Jackson hadn't wanted her enough to remain, and yet he was trying to ruin what he thought she had with another man. Mallory turned on him.

"If there's trouble, you're the one who's trying to stir it up, Jackson."

He hated when she came to this phantom Steven's defense. Hated it more than he thought possible. "You make me sound like the devil." He stuck out his boot-shod foot. "Look, no cloven hoof." Jackson moved toward her on the sofa, knowing he could never be close enough to her to satisfy himself. "The only cleft I have is in my chin." He stuck it out.

Going with sudden impulse, Mallory swung and clipped it. When he looked at her in complete amazement, she shrugged and had the good grace to be embarrassed, "Sorry, maybe I'm overreacting."

He rubbed his chin, more surprised than hurt. "Yeah, maybe. What about your, um, other problem?"" His eyes slid down to her breasts.

She shrugged, frustration eating away at her. "I'm fine. All systems go." Restlessness began to take hold. Rising, she felt as if she had to leave. It was as if she sensed a storm coming. But the sky outside was clear. "I just can't seem to produce milk. She says these things happen."

He studied her expression. "You don't look as if you're convinced."

"I'm not." She blew out a breath. Sheila's words notwithstanding, she was still having trouble coming to terms with her feelings of inadequacy. "I feel like a failure."

That sounded illogical to him. "Why, because you can't produce a little milk?"

A rueful smile twitched on her lips. "You make it sound silly." She didn't know whether to laugh or be annoyed at his tone.

"It is." He thought of the baby upstairs, the one who was swiftly burrowing his way into his heart. "The thing Joshua needs most is your love. That and to be changed regularly."

She laughed softly, some of her tension dissipating. "That's what the doctor said. Except for the changing part," she amended.

"Wise woman."

He'd only met Dr. Pollack that one time in the delivery room, but what he had seen had impressed him. She struck him as a very capable, efficient woman.

Coming up behind Mallory, he placed his hands on her shoulders in mute comfort. "Why don't you do yourself a favor and listen to her?"

He was touching her again. Whisking away what passed for her brains and leaving mincemeat in its place, like a magpie making a trade.

She turned around to face him. All she had managed to do was succeed in getting Jackson to shift his hands to her arms.

"I know I should." She loved him touching her like this. Just holding her and making her feel all those wonderful sensations she always did in his arms.

But it wasn't like that for them anymore. She wasn't falling in love for the first time. She was a woman who'd been there and back. She'd seen the underbelly of love, the rough side after it was all over. She'd held the ashes in her hands and wept.

She was never going through that again.

Bracing her shoulders, Mallory stiffened but couldn't quite make herself pull away. "You're breaking rule number two," she murmured.

"Bending it a little," he corrected. "Just this once." Because he couldn't help himself, he ran his hands along her bare arms. "You look as if you need someone to hold you right now." He pressed her closer to himself, absorbing the warmth of her body into his own. "And I'm volunteering."

More than volunteering, he thought, getting lost in the scent and feel of her.

He felt her shaking against him. "Mallory?" He tilted her head back. His heart quickened as his suspicions were confirmed. "You're crying."

She shrugged, self-conscious. Quickly, she wiped away the evidence. More arrived to take its place. "Just hormones bouncing around again."

"I know what you mean," he said softly. Lowering his head, Jackson kissed one tear away as it slid down her cheek. "Hard things to tame, hormones." Lightly, he pressed his lips to her other cheek. He tasted her. "Salty," he murmured.

Her heart was lodged in her throat, throbbing. Her eyes were fixed on his face. "Tears always are," she said thickly.

"I've always been a sucker for salt."

Fingers pressed to the long, slim column of her throat he gently tilted her head back again. His mouth found hers. And he found his redemption.

Jackson could feel her heart thudding against his chest. The beat was no less erratic than his own. Soon, it began to feel as if it were all one and the same. Two joined to form one.

Oh, how he'd missed her, missed her with every fiber of his being.

Desire exploded in his veins. Exercising extreme control, Jackson harnessed it just enough to contain his ardor.

But not enough to draw away from her.

It was like coming into the light after months of wandering around within a tunnel. He had to come closer to the light, had to be able to see again, to bathe himself in its life-giving warmth. If there were penalties to be paid, he'd pay them, pay them all. Anything just to have her again.

A moan escaped her lips as Jackson deepened the kiss. She meant to push him away, to form a wedge between them with her hands. But she couldn't make them work properly. Instead of pushing him away, they betrayed her, rallying with her feelings instead of her head. Her arms went around his neck, holding on to him for dear life.

For suddenly, life had become dear.

And still the kiss deepened. Deepened like a giant crevice, opening up beneath her feet and engulfing her until there was no floor below, no ceiling above. Nothing at all but the kiss.

And Jackson.

She could feel his hands, his wonderful, clever hands sliding over her body, molding her to him. The heat of his own pervaded her, making her ache for him the way she had in the loneliness of those long nights she'd spent without him.

It was just like the first time, she thought. No, more. It was more exciting, more intense because of the lack, of the long, dry period where only dreams had sustained her.

She wanted him more than she wanted anything else in her life. If it was madness to leave herself open this way, then all right, she was mad. Temporarily insane. They granted reprieves for people who were temporarily insane, didn't they?

She'd look for a reprieve later.

Right now, all she wanted was this. This wonderful sensation that lifted her up to the sky and made her feel whole again. Made her feel loved again. Only Jackson had done that. Only Jackson had made her feel loved, precious, fulfilled.

*And only Jackson had managed to take it away,* a small voice whispered on the perimeter of her mind. *Take it away swiftly, without mercy.*

Mallory banished the small voice from her consciousness. She couldn't think now. Only later.

Damn it, he was behaving like some kind of animal, pawing her. He hated that image, hated the fact that he seemed to have such little control over himself.

With a shaky breath, he pulled back. If nothing else, he could at least warn her. "Mallory, I'm not going to be able to stop in another moment."

It was past the time for warnings. Past the time for stopping. Her lips blurred from the imprint of his, her eyes smoky, she shook her head.

"Then don't."

With the last bit of strength available to him, Jackson held her at arm's length. "Mallory, you just had a baby."

A smile bloomed on her face as she took his face between her hands. Lord, but she loved this man.

"Two weeks ago." She swallowed, knowing she was signing her own death sentence. Not caring. "The doctor said I was fine," Mallory assured him. "It's okay to have relations."

She couldn't bring herself to say "sex." She didn't want to think of it as that. Sex was barren, naked, a cold-eyed, scheming woman, devoid of love. And at least she loved, Mallory thought. That made it different.

Jackson looked at her, stunned. "You asked her about it?"

"Not outright, but that was the general implication." Needing to skim her lips along his skin, to lose herself in the dark, musky tastes and smells that were his alone, Mallory pressed a kiss to his throat.

And signed both their futures away.

She felt his hands tighten on her arms, gripping them. Felt his body stiffen and shudder just a little. Felt him become hers again, at least for a little while.

It was enough. It would have to be.

A sense of power surged through her and she let it take her away.

He meant to give her one more chance. Chivalry had raised its shining head from somewhere, where he didn't know. She'd always managed to bring out the best in him that way.

But not this time. Not completely. His need for her consumed him to such an extent that he couldn't just back away.

Not if his life depended on it. Because it depended on just the opposite.

Chivalry died a quick death.

His lips traced the outline of her face slowly, relearning the terrain like a blind man forced to touch a surface in order to visualize it in his mind again. Jackson felt his fingers fumbling at the buttons on her blouse, trying to undo them. They were fumbling like a young boy's on the brink of his first time.

And maybe with her it was, he conceded. Because Mallory made him feel the way no other woman ever had. The way no other woman ever would.

She made him feel protective and needy all at the same time. A knight in shining armor pledging himself to Guenivere. A supplicant at the back door, hoping to be admitted.

She made him feel everything, made him experience a spectrum of sensations that had never been available to him before, except in her arms, in her bed.

In her body.

Mallory gasped as his hands cupped her breasts. Her nipples hardened instantly beneath the thin material, straining for more. Hands on his shoulders, Mallory arched, pressing herself into his hands, desperately wanting more.

She couldn't have done anything more erotic if she'd rehearsed it. The simple act of offering herself to him fueled the desire already racing in his veins like an Indianapolis 500 stock car around the track, making it burn bright.

It was all he could do not to rip away her clothes, to plunge himself into her and take her this moment. The desire that had been resurrected, full-bodied and demanding within him had turned into a beast of tremendous proportions. Keeping it in check, keeping it from frightening her, was almost more than Jackson was capable of.

But he had to be. For Mallory's sake. She deserved more than to be taken like some Viking peasant, quickly and without thought.

He wanted her to remember this. When she thought again of Steven, or of living a tranquil and placid life beside the man, Jackson wanted her to remember this. And ache for him.

More than that, he wanted her to return to him and remain.

Jackson's mouth felt hot as it raced along her face and throat. His hands were demanding as they roamed over her body. And yet, beneath the fire, there was a gentleness to him that made her want to cry.

He wanted her. Wanted her the way she ached to be wanted. And he made her feel like all things. Beautiful, capable of leaping tall buildings on a single bound. Of flying unaided by such mundane things as airplanes or parachutes.

He gave her wings and she soared.

More than that, with the simple press of his lips to hers, he made her feel as if she were home again. And home was a wondrous palace that spread before her to be endlessly explored.

# Eight

He felt clumsy, harnessed by the very desire that begged to be freed, afraid that if he released it, it would consume them both.

And yet if he didn't release it, Jackson thought he would explode.

Drawing a deep breath, he held Mallory away from him. He could taste her, on his lips, on his very soul. And he wanted more. So much more. But it had to be what she wanted, too.

"I think I should warn you."

Mallory looked up at him, hearing him through a barrier of haze, warm passion in her eyes.

"What?" What could he possibly have to warn her about that she hadn't already covered herself? Covered and discarded.

He could devour her whole right here, right now, he thought. How could he have ever thought that he had the upper hand in this relationship? The cards were all hers.

"I've been celibate for over eight months."

"You?" She uttered the word incredulously, staring at him. He couldn't expect her to believe that. When they'd been together, they'd made love almost every day. It didn't seem possible that someone as sensual, as passionate as Jackson would have willingly refrained from making love for so long.

"Yeah." Jackson cupped his hands about her face, content for the moment just to steep himself in the very sight and feel of her. "Me." How could he make her understand and still retain a little bit of his pride? How could he tell her what he was feeling and still remain a man? But wanting her had stripped away everything else he'd once thought defined who and what he was. "There were women, but I just couldn't go through with it. Couldn't make love with them. No one else seemed worth bothering with after you."

Why had he left, then? It didn't make sense, none of it. Unless she thought of it as just another story he was creating.

It didn't have to make sense.

Right now, the knowledge that no other woman had been with him by his own choice warmed and aroused her beyond belief.

Never mind that it didn't matter. Never mind that he would leave her again because men like Jackson couldn't remain tied down for long. She had right now and she would make the most of it.

Her body ached for him. Like a dormant instrument left in a corner ached to play a haunting melody just one more time, she ached for him.

If he didn't make love with her right now, she was afraid she wouldn't be able to pick up all the pieces that would be left.

She touched his cheek with her hand, her breath warm and enticing upon his face. An invitation to a far better place than he had known of late. "Then you have a lot of catching up to do."

It was all he needed.

Jackson filled his hands with her hair, his fingers pressed against the back of her head, urging her closer to him as his mouth roamed over the planes of her face. Anointing her, arousing her. Reclaiming her.

Her breath caught in her throat as she shivered. The excitement he generated within her was indescribable. It felt as if she'd been sleeping all this time, as if she hadn't really been alive all these last months. Until this very moment.

With shaking fingers, she tore at the buttons on his shirt. She wanted to touch him, to feel him against her heated skin again. She needed to feel him to convince herself that this wasn't some apparition that had come to her in the night, but really Jackson. Jackson by daylight.

She was going too quickly, undermining the last shreds of his control. He stopped her hands as they moved, butterfly quick, over his chest.

"Do you want to go to bed?" he murmured against her mouth.

He had to ask? "Yes."

Running her tongue along her lips, Mallory could taste his words. Taste the hunger there. It stoked her own.

Jackson bent down to pick her up in his arms, but she shook her head. She thought he'd uttered a euphemism for lovemaking, not a physical location. She didn't want to go upstairs with him. It was far too great a journey and she was far too impatient to make it.

"No, here. On the sofa."

Like the first time, Mallory thought. The first time that they had made love, Jackson had taken her here, on the sofa, multicolored cushions scattered every which way beneath them. They'd only known each other a short while. It was one of those relationships that was destined from the start to be consummated.

They'd spent the entire night on the sofa, never making it upstairs at all. That had been the first time. It seemed somehow fitting that they should make love here the last time as well.

She wouldn't think of that. Refused to think of that. No last times. She had this moment and it was going to have to be enough. She was going to have to be satisfied.

*Just once more,* her body whispered in supplication. *Love me just once more and I'll make it last forever.*

She wanted to wrap herself around him, her body trembling as he slowly slid the sleeves of her blouse down her arms. Impatience hammered a desperate tattoo through her, her loins readying in anticipation. She'd waited so long for this, never knowing if it was going to happen again.

If it was weak to give in to the pounding needs that begged to be freed, then she was weak. But oh, she had missed being held this way, being kissed this way, as if she were the only one in the world. The only one in the world to be loved like this.

For during these moments, Mallory knew he loved her. Loved her as much as Jackson Cain was capable of loving anyone or anything. He was giving her everything he had to give.

No one could ask for more than that.

Tenderness and rapture twined as she gave herself up to the paradise that only he could create.

They undressed each other with familiarity framed with the reverent wonder that distance and time bred. Her blouse fell on the floor, to be covered with his shirt. Her bra floated on top a moment later.

She saw the flame of desire flare higher in his eyes as they swept over her and could have cried with joy. It was the same look that had been there before, but it burned with a brighter intensity.

Jackson slid his hands along her body, reclaiming what had once been his, damning the thought of another man ever having taken his place.

Damning himself for having silently allowed it with his absence.

*Like cream, like sweet cream,* he thought. Her skin felt like cream beneath his palms and he wanted nothing more than to fill himself with cream.

Passion's wings beating within him like twin engines of an airborne plane, Jackson glided his hands down along her hips. He delved his long fingers on either side of her hips beneath her panties.

She still wore the skimpiest excuse for underwear imaginable, he thought with a sensual smile. The sight and feel of the satiny scrap excited him further, sending his blood into a fever pitch.

He nearly tore them off as he slid the pink undergarments down her legs, all the while his mouth doing wicked things to her body.

Mallory gasped as she felt the light sting of air whirling around her buttocks. A moment later, the soft breeze was replaced by the hot touch of his hands. Kneading her pliant flesh, he molded her to him. She felt the throbbing rhythm of his desire as he pressed against her.

He was hard from wanting her.

She nearly broke the zipper on his jeans in her struggle to rid them both of the denim barrier between them.

She was sweet in her eagerness, Jackson thought. It nearly undid him. In the face of her ardor, his own nearly spilled over the top.

Any easy, flippant words on his tongue disappeared, evaporated in the heat of his desire. The intensity of it would have scared the hell out of him all those months ago. *Had* scared the hell out of him eight months ago.

But now it gladdened his heart and made him feel alive for the first time in all those months.

How could he have ever fooled himself into thinking that he could have stayed away from this, from her, and gone on living? She hadn't stolen his passion, she *was* his passion.

His fingers played upon her body with a raging intensity that was still harnessed in the very last vestiges of restraint and tenderness. He gloried in the familiarity, in the easy sensuality that was ripe for his plucking.

Intimately, his fingers dipped between her legs. Her eyes flew open in surprised wonder. As he watched her face, his fingers whispered along the very perimeter of her longing, bringing her instantly to a peak.

He felt her stiffen, clutching at his shoulders for support, and then gasping out his name. But the gasp turned into a moan as he worked her up and over the next peak. And the next.

Mallory shuddered, arching into his hand, silently begging for more, weakened by the last climax and urged on by it at the same time.

No one *ever* made her feel the way he did. And no one ever would. She knew that with the same certainty that she knew the passing of the seasons.

Hungrily, her mouth devoured his. As Mallory fed from him, she broke the last bands of any restraint he had left available to him.

Naked, clothed in each other, they fell upon the sofa, limbs tangled in an intimate knot. Rolling, shifting, they rolled off and onto the floor.

Neither noticed. It was too insignificant a thing to take note of, consumed as they were in the rapture that had been reopened to them.

His body was slick with her desire, as well as his own anticipation. The feel of it upon his body urged him on like a silent rallying cry.

He wanted to take her in a hundred different ways, wanted to prolong this as long as he could. Wanted to take her now, this moment.

Desire almost succeeded in tearing him apart.

His, she was his. Never mind if her body had borne another man's child. Never mind if she'd lain with someone else while he had spent sleepless nights, dreaming of her a continent away. She was his.

Every fiber of his body felt it. She couldn't react to him this way if she belonged to someone else. She was no man's but his.

The thought empowered him even as it humbled him and brought him to his knees in grateful worship.

Jackson called himself a fool for ever having run from this.

Hungry for her, for release, for sustenance, his mouth roamed her body, grazing it with hot, openmouthed kisses that made her writhe and twist beneath him, crying out his name. Hearing her, feeling her, pushed him on.

The imprint of his mouth upon her quivering belly stoked the fires burning along her flesh. His kisses only ignited them further. When his tongue found her, flickering in and out as lightly as a hummingbird, she bit her lip to keep from crying out in ecstasy.

In the throes of sweet agony, she burned for him, for the joining that made her whole again.

Moving urgently under him, Mallory grasped Jackson's arms and tried to pull him up to her level. Feeling his body rub against hers made her tremble with anticipation.

"Now, Jackson. Now."

He would have laughed and said it was the best offer he'd had in a long time if he were able. If he could talk. But wanting her had closed off all words, all ability to speak. His throat felt tight with desire.

Instead, he slid his body along hers until their very faces were level. With the last ounce of tenderness he had at his disposal, Jackson framed her face in his hands. His eyes watching hers intently, he slowly sheathed himself in her.

He'd come home.

The greeting was instantaneous. Hips sealed to one another, they rode the lengthening peaks together in search of higher ground. She arched and bucked, he set the pace. The ride was swift, furious and over with all too soon.

They crossed the finish line together.

Exhausted beyond comprehension, Jackson struggled not to pin her with his entire weight. Pivoting some of the weight onto his elbows, he wondered where the hidden cache of strength had materialized from. He hadn't thought he had enough left to whisper his own name.

If he could have remembered it.

For a second, he was content just to feel her heart beating wildly beneath his. The erratic rhythm matched his own.

The thought was comforting. Now that the euphoria was clearing away, it was nice to know that he wasn't alone in this.

Tears of joy sprang up in her eyes, mingling indiscriminately with tears of regret. The one outweighed the other.

She shouldn't have done that, she thought, sorrow opening up like a black hole, waiting to swallow her up. The break was going to be harder on her now. So much harder. And it was sure to come.

Nothing in the world, not even the passion she'd just felt, the passion she'd both experienced and received, could convince her that Jackson wasn't going to leave again. He'd done it once, when she would have sworn to anyone with ears to hear that everything was perfect between them. Now things weren't so perfect. Nothing was going to keep him here.

He raised himself up on his elbows, kissing her lightly on the forehead. Jackson looked around, as if just now becoming aware of his surroundings.

"We fell." He nodded toward the sofa, a smile playing lightly along his lips.

Mallory lay on the carpet, her hair pooled about her head. She brushed aside a strand that had fallen into her eyes. Closing them, she sighed.

"Yes, I did."

He didn't like the way she said that, not "we," but "I," as if it had been a regrettable incident. He didn't want her to regret this.

Leaning over, Jackson pressed a kiss to her neck and felt her stiffening instead of giving beneath him. Rolling off, he gathered his thoughts together and looked at her.

"What's the matter?"

She turned her head and looked away. Remorse arrived in a horse-drawn carriage far more quickly than she had anticipated. Mallory pressed her lips together. "Nothing."

Taking her chin in his hand, he forced her to look at him. Regret. He saw it in her eyes. *Damn.*

"Don't tell me 'nothing.' You look confused, bewildered." His voice was low, forbidding her to utter what he saw in her eyes. He didn't think he could stand it if she did.

Suddenly cold, Mallory reached up to the sofa and pulled one of the pillows down to her. Positioned strategically, it was just enough to cover her. But not enough to banish the chill. Maybe nothing ever would.

"Why shouldn't I be?" Afraid she was going to cry again, she purposely maintained a light tone. "Dorothy probably felt less confusion during the tornado ride that took her to Oz."

He grinned, playing his hand along her hip. Her belly was almost completely flat. It amazed him that only two weeks ago, it had been round with a child. Her skin was incredibly resilient. But then, it belonged to a very special lady.

"Is that where you went, Mallory? To Oz?" He'd like to think that he did that to her, robbed her of her orientation until she didn't know where she was, or who. She certainly did that to him.

Mallory sighed again. Her words came out on a shaky breath. "It certainly wasn't any place I've ever been to before. Not even with you."

That was good, he thought, right? But he needed more. "Not even with Steven?"

She'd give him that small crumb. It didn't seem fair otherwise. "Not even with Steven."

Suddenly unable to put up with the lies, Mallory sat up abruptly, reaching for her clothes. They were scattered like dust motes about the coffee table.

There was something in the set of her shoulders that alerted him. Something distant and foreign. A barrier rising up between them again. Sitting up, Jackson caught her arm and made her turn toward him.

He wanted to clear the air. And clear away an obstacle. "That was me you made love with, Mallory, not Steven." She had to be made to see that she didn't love Steven. She loved him.

"I know that." She raised her chin. "But it was a mistake."

The solitary word throbbed between them, tearing holes into him, hurting him as if it had been fashioned out of cacti spines. He set his jaw. The outline where she'd pressed kisses only minutes before turned rigid.

"What, you thought I was Steven? I thought some parts might have been recognizable to you." Bitterness filled his mouth like the foul taste of bile. "Should I have shown you some I.D. before I undressed you?"

"No." With all the dignity she could muster, she rose, her head held high. "I just shouldn't have made love with you, that's all. That's the mistake."

She bit her lip. It was so hard to go on with this lie, but the lie was all she had to protect her from succumbing completely and making a total fool of herself. That was the way she felt the first time, like a fool to have loved him so much that she couldn't think straight when he had felt nothing. It had to have been nothing for Jackson to have been able to just walk away from her like that.

She cleared her throat and tried to say something that made sense. Everything was tangling in her head like the threads of an unraveling patchwork quilt. Logic dueled with emotion for possession of her soul.

And throughout it all, she still wanted him again. "Steven—"

"Oh, the hell with Steven," Jackson shouted. He rose up to his feet, taking her up with him. "I know you, Mallory. You wouldn't have been able to make love with me if you loved this Steven character."

To keep her from turning away, he captured her shoulders between his hands. When she winced, he realized that he had squeezed too tightly. He had to will himself to release her, hoping that his words would hold her in place instead.

"You're not like that. What is there between the two of you?" he demanded. He knew it wasn't love. It couldn't be. Her love belonged to him. She only had to be made to see that.

Tears shone in Mallory's eyes. She told him the single thing that she had wished with all her heart had existed between the two of them.

"Commitment."

"Some commitment." He sneered at the word. "You were carrying his child and he didn't even marry you."

"What do you know about it?" she snapped. Mallory's mind scrambled to piece together a coherent story. Neat trick, that, she thought, when her mind was turning to mush. "He would have." Momentum built in her voice as the words formed. "He wanted to."

Not good enough, Jackson thought. Like a magnificent god in his nakedness, completely oblivious to it, his arms folded before him, Jackson stood in judgment of the missing man. "But?"

"I don't have to explain Steven to you," she retorted hotly.

"But?" he repeated expectantly with more feeling.

The sigh was ragged. She was cornered, but she wasn't going down. "I already told you. I didn't want Steven doing anything out of a sense of obligation. I wanted it to be out of love."

"So? He doesn't love you?" Suddenly, it became crystal clear to him. Of course, why hadn't he seen it before? She'd gone to Steven on the rebound. That had to be it.

She was leaving the room. Hurrying after her, Jackson caught her by the arm and moved to face her. He had to see her face, had to see it in her eyes to be sure. "Or is it that you don't love him?"

She tried to stare him down, her insides quaking like gelatin being lobbed over a tennis net. "He's good, and kind, and treats me with respect."

That wasn't what he'd asked. "All good qualities, but I'm talking about love, Mallory. Love. Do you love him?"

She had no course open to her. She gave in to the last lie, the greatest one of all. "Yes."

His eyes darkened. The woman he'd just taken on the floor didn't love anyone else. She loved him. "I don't believe you."

Mallory pulled her arm free with a jerk. "Then that's your problem."

The momentary silence between them was broken by a small cry floating down the stairs.

*Thank you, Joshua. Thank you for saving your mother.*

Her face a mask of frozen indignation, she looked at Jackson. "Now, if you'll excuse me, I have my son to tend to. Thank you for staying with him while I went to the doctor."

He didn't trust himself to answer her. Instead, he turned his back on Mallory as he quickly pulled on his clothes. It was only after a beat that he turned around and saw her walking from the room, her own clothing still piled up in her hands.

From where he stood, Jackson could see Mallory mount the stairs, a nude, regal princess cloaked in her own dignity.

He was angry, furious really, and yet, he still wanted her. That was probably his sentence for having left her in the first place, he thought miserably. He was going to be damned to the fires of hell for all eternity, wanting her.

Well, he was a long way off from dead yet, he thought. And as the trite saying went, where there was life, there was hope. And while Steven was gone, Jackson intended to make a strong case for himself.

He already knew she loved him. She just had to be convinced to keep on loving him. And he was nothing if not persuasive.

At least, he thought, he fervently hoped so.

# Nine

———

Mallory pushed the baby carriage into the house and shut the door behind her with her shoulder. She'd taken Joshua out for a walk. She'd intended for it to be a brisk fifteen or twenty minute walk around a couple of residential blocks. But after yesterday, and Jackson, her head needed clearing. Before she knew it, she'd walked out of the development, through the next one and down to the main road that connected one end of Bedford to the other.

It was one of those typical, gorgeous California mornings. The brisk wind had cleared away the smog and the smattering of white clouds scattered throughout the crystal blue sky looked as if they all were hand painted bits of cotton.

But Mallory was more interested in the terrain she covered than the sky above. The real estate agent in her took over as she mentally catalogued all the houses that were up for sale, noting the new ones that had been placed on the market in the last two weeks.

It took only a moment for her to realize just how much she missed her work. To her, it was more than just a job. It was a way of bringing people together with their dreams. To her each home was the physical embodiment of a dream come true. A dream that would continue to come true for the family who lived within it. A new house, no matter what the age, always represented endless possibilities. Walls that could come down, rooms that could be enlarged. A study turned into a den, a den becoming a nursery, as hers had. With imagination and energy, there was no end to the options.

She took special pride in bringing together people with just the right house. One they might have otherwise thought beyond their means, but for some clever refinagling of finances between owners new and old, escrow companies and second trust deed loans.

Each and every potential sale was a challenge to her and she missed that.

Not that she didn't exactly have a challenge of her own to face right now, she thought as she had turned the carriage back toward home.

She'd met Jackson that way, she remembered with a bittersweet pang. He'd come to her to lease a house. Not buy, lease. That should have been her very first clue to run for the hills.

But the hills had gotten farther and farther away, she thought with a sigh. Even after he'd leased the house, she hadn't been able to stop seeing him.

Leaning against the door, she looked down at Joshua. Her son's cheeks were glowing and pink from the brush of the breeze. "Well, you look like you had a good time," she murmured as she picked him up.

Jackson entered from the kitchen. Her pulse quickened instantly. She'd been hoping to get up to the nursery without running into him. Since yesterday, they'd hardly exchanged more than five sentences. Each time he looked as if he wanted to say something, she'd found an excuse to abruptly leave the room.

She was running out of excuses.

She should just tell him to leave, she thought. But it wasn't that easy. Trying to pretend that nothing had happened was even harder.

Jackson bit down on the apple in his hand, watching her. Her movements were short, abrupt. Mallory looked like a rabbit at the beginning of hunting season.

Pursuit, now there was a new one on him. He'd never had to pursue anyone. For him it had always been a matter of just standing still and letting women lavish their attention on him. This was certainly different for him, he mused.

He felt as if he were trying to lay boards across quicksand and work his way to shore before the boards were sucked up into the muck. "You had a telephone call while you were out."

She'd been about to leave the room when his words stopped her. Damn it, what was wrong with her? This was her house. If anyone was going to any leaving, it was going to be him, not her.

She turned around and looked at Jackson. "Who?"

Jackson perched on the arm of the sofa, still eating. She had absolutely no idea why watching his lips making contact with the apple's skin could be so hopelessly erotic to her.

"Steven." He watched her eyes for any telltale signs. "He said he loves Alaska so much that he's decided to stay on as an advisor at the plant."

Mallory sat down on the love seat and slipped off Joshua's yellow jacket from his arms. She looked accusingly at Jackson. "Steven didn't call."

His smile, casual and sultry, challenged her. "How do you know that?"

He was becoming more and more convinced that there was no Steven. That for some reason, Mallory had made the man up and was only clinging to her story to maintain the barrier between them.

But why? They were so good together. He was willing to make amends. Why wouldn't she let him?

"Because Steven wouldn't say something like that," she informed him coolly. "When I talked to him earlier, he said he couldn't wait to come back." She hedged her bets a little further. "Except that there was a foul-up and he might have to remain longer." She pinned him with a look. "But not indefinitely. And he hates the cold. I can't even get him to go skiing in the winter. So living in Alaska would be out of the question."

Jackson shrugged. He got up to throw out the apple core, then returned. There was almost a little boy look on his face. "Can't blame a guy for trying."

Tiny bubbles formed around Joshua's mouth. Jackson leaned over and plucked a tissue out of the dispenser on the coffee table. He offered it to Mallory, indicating the baby's face.

"Funny you should mention staying longer," he began nonchalantly.

She looked up sharply, alert. Now what was he up to? "Yes?" Mallory wiped her son's mouth and then rose.

Jackson was on his feet beside her. This was the longest conversation they'd had since she had walked out of the living room, nude. He didn't intend for it to end quickly.

"My research isn't going as well as I'd hoped it would." All the research he needed to do could be handled via telephone, but she didn't have to know that. "It looks like I'm going to have to stay a few days longer than first planned." He watched her face for any indication that she was glad he had to stay the extra time.

She felt the incline she was on growing steeper, threatening to make her slip and fall. "Don't get too comfortable," she warned. "You have to be gone before Steven gets back from his trip."

"Why?" He stuck his tongue in his cheek. "I thought Steven doesn't have a jealous bone in his body."

Her eyes narrowed. "He doesn't, but I don't want to push it."

"Lucky for me, his trip's been extended," Jackson commented. "That gives me a little leeway."

And none for me, she thought. Determined to get a little space between them, she picked up Joshua's jacket and hat from the love seat and turned to leave.

Restlessness moved through him like a dog unable to find a spot on the rug where he could settle down. He touched her arm and felt her stiffen immediately. Damn, what did it take for her to forgive him? he wondered. "Mallory, we have to talk."

There was a new one, she thought cryptically. Jackson wanted to talk and she didn't. She didn't want to talk with him because she was afraid he'd seduce her with words just as effectively as he had with his body yesterday. Maybe even more so.

She didn't want to be seduced, didn't want to start believing in what really didn't have a chance of ever happening.

Actions spoke louder than words and Jackson had already acted. He'd left her once. He'd do it again. She'd pushed that cold fact to the side yesterday, but things looked different to her once passion had returned to a low, continuous sizzle.

"No, we don't."

She began to leave. Jackson shifted in front of her, blocking her way. "All right, can I write you a note then?"

Mallory didn't like being cornered and absolutely hated feeling as if she had no control over her own destiny. He did that to her, took it right out of her hands and into his own. It wasn't fair.

"This isn't funny, Jackson."

"No, it's not," he readily agreed, his tone growing more serious. "But I'm looking for a way to get into the subject with you."

Her eyes, he thought, could have frosted over hell at ten paces, but he stood his ground. He had no choice.

"I think you got into it enough yesterday," she retorted.

Jackson struggled to hold on to his temper. It wouldn't help matters to shout at her, though he wanted to. Was she implying that he had forced himself on her? He'd done everything in his power not to, to give her a way out if she wanted to take it, even though it would have probably killed him if she had.

His eyes were dark, like storm clouds before a deluge. "You're saying you didn't want yesterday to happen?"

She wasn't going to get angry, she wasn't, Mallory swore to herself. She wasn't going to raise her voice around her son. But it wasn't easy.

"I'm saying I wanted it to happen too much. I don't need old wounds opening up." Couldn't he understand that?

She knew better than to think he'd just obey her, he thought. He'd felt her reaction. She wanted him as much as he wanted her. Why couldn't she accept that? And him?

"I think we're a few steps past 'wanting' and smack-dab into 'having.'" He ran his hand along her arm gently, positively.

Mallory shrugged him off. She didn't want to discuss it. She could pretend yesterday had never happened if she ignored it. After all, wasn't that his way? He had managed to ignore a full four months of "happenings" between them when he'd left.

She shifted Joshua to her shoulder, tucking his outerwear under her arm. "I have to get upstairs and change him before he turns ripe."

Jackson sniffed the air. "Too late. By the way," he went on as if she hadn't just attempted to cut him away from her like unwanted barnacles from the bottom of a hull. "You really did get a phone call." He followed her up the stairs and into the nursery. "Someone named Ursula. She said your couple bought the Melville place."

Mallory placed her son on the changing table. She looked at Jackson over her shoulder, her eyes bright. For a moment, the fencing match between them was forgotten. "Really?"

Why couldn't she look like that when he tried to talk to her about them? It would come, he promised himself. It would come.

Making himself useful, Jackson took a diaper out of the box against the wall and put it beside Joshua on the table. "Would I make something like that up? I take it that it's your listing." The woman on the telephone had sounded pretty excited. Apparently, the Melville house had been a white elephant that had languished on a market already crammed full of houses.

Mallory made short work of the aromatic diaper. As she wiped his bottom, Joshua kicked his fat legs in glee. "Yes, it is."

Jackson held up the wastebasket for her. She deposited the dirty, disposable diaper. He replaced the lid, curtailing the odor. "Congratulations. I guess this is an occasion to celebrate."

*Oh-oh.* Leeriness filled her eyes. "I don't think that I have time to—"

Another rejection. He didn't want to hear it. A man's ego could only take so much in a day. He made a counter move, cutting Mallory short. "Why don't I finish changing Joshua for you?" He was already edging her out and taking over her space.

She stepped back. He did that rather well, she thought grudgingly. "You don't have to."

"No, really, it's okay." Mallory stood watching him as he powdered Joshua's bottom. "Joshua and I are getting to be old friends. Aren't we, Josh?"

Jackson smiled down at the tiny human being cooing and waving his feet on the changing table. He glanced up at Mallory. She had that same odd expression on her face as she watched him, he realized. The one he couldn't quite read.

He continued as if he didn't notice. "You know, I never thought about having kids. My parents did such a botched up job of creating a family atmosphere that I never really thought about starting a family of my own." He closed the tabs on the diaper and tested them to make sure that they held. "It seemed a lot simpler just to travel through life by myself. But after Josh here—" He tickled the baby under his chin. More bubbles sprouted from his rosebud mouth. Jackson cleaned him off and picked Joshua up. "I kind of like the idea." He cradled the baby against him. It really did feel right, he mused. "One or two kids could be nice."

Mallory took her son from him, trying not to think about the fact that Joshua was *their* son and not just hers. "Where would you keep them?"

Jackson looked at her, confused. "In my back pocket," he quipped. "What do you mean, where would I keep them? Where does anyone keep their children?"

That answer was for normal people. Jackson's life-style wasn't normal. He was a nomad. "Well, you never settle down. You lease a house, stay for a while and then pick up and go away." She turned to face him, daring him to refute what she was saying. "You told me yourself that it was a pattern."

*And I was fool enough to think I could change you.*

He wound a lock of her hair around his finger, his eyes on hers. Jackson felt his way slowly along shaky ground. "I could change, given the right conditions."

She'd been down that road before. Mallory jerked the strand away from him, wishing that she could pull her heart away as easily.

Did he think she was stupid, or just slow? "Yeah, right." She left him behind as she walked downstairs again.

Undeterred, Jackson followed her into the family room. "Don't you believe me?"

Mallory placed Joshua into the suspended Portacrib near the window and cranked the handle. Slowly, the mesh-sided crib began to sway in time with "Mary Had a Little Lamb."

"No."

He wondered how long he was going to have to atone for his stupidity. "Then I guess I'll just have to convince you."

Positioning the Port a crib so that she could see it from the kitchen, Mallory crossed the room and went to the refrigerator. "I don't see how."

It was difficult building a case for himself with a moving target. He remained in the family room, watching Joshua slowly swing back and forth.

Tiny hands and feet were aloft, kicking madly as if he were practicing how to run. He was going to be some handful when he learned how to walk, Jackson mused.

"Well, then, I—" Jackson raised his voice so that Mallory could hear him. The telephone rang, interrupting them.

She jumped at the opportunity to table the discussion. "Get that for me, will you, Jackson?" She took out a can of formula and opened it. "I have my hands full."

He didn't want to talk to someone else, he wanted to talk to her. "The machine'll pick it up." He went to the kitchen doorway, unable to resist getting in a little dig. "Aren't you afraid that it might be Steven and he'll be jealous?"

"Just pick it up for me, all right?" She filled three small bottles and screwed the tops back on. "It might be important."

What was important was that he leave the room, and the narrow path his argument was taking. She didn't want to be convinced that there might be a chance for them. She already knew that there wasn't.

Acquiescing, Jackson retreated to answer the telephone. He managed to get to it on its last ring, just as the answering machine clicked on.

"Hold it," he warned the person on the other end. "Mallory wants me to take this call for her, so stay on the line."

*And if this is Steven, I hope you're calling from an ice-
berg and that you're floating out to sea. Or hell, whichev-
er'll keep you permanently away.*

He was getting irrational, Jackson thought. But then, this
wasn't exactly a run-of-the mill situation for him. He was in
love with his ex-girlfriend *and* her baby. More than anything, he wanted to find a way back into something he had
blatantly walked out on.

Ran out on, he corrected himself silently as he listened to
Mallory's recorded voice cheerfully ask for a message as well
as the best time that she could return the call.

"Hi?" a low, sultry voice inquired on the other end of the
line after the low beep had sounded.

Once upon a time, the sound of a sexy voice would have
had him creating an image in his mind to match. Now all he
could think about was the woman in the other room, preparing baby bottles.

"Hello. Mallory's busy with the baby. Can I take a message?"

And who was this? Nicole Lincoln wondered. The last
time she'd spoken to Mallory, the other woman was cheerfully facing her pregnancy alone and swearing that she liked
it that way. Obviously not, Nicole smiled to herself. She
fingered the birth announcement she'd received Monday.

"Yes, a quick one. Tell her that Nicole Lincoln called to
congratulate her on the birth of her son and that I'm absolutely crazy about the house." She thought of Dennis. "We
both are. And to look for an invitation in today's mail."

Jackson could have sworn he heard the sound of wails in
the background, like a baby crying except that it was in
stereo. He glanced toward the family room, but Joshua was
busy sucking on his fist. The sound had to be coming from
the telephone.

"Ooops, I guess I'd better go," Nicole said with a laugh.
"I'm being summoned. Tell Mallory that I'll be in touch.
And not to skip out on the invitation. I won't take no for an
answer. 'Bye."

"'Bye." The other end of the line had gone dead. Jackson hung up.

"Who was it?" Mallory asked. Bottle in hand she picked Joshua up and sat down on the L-shaped sofa that surrounded the huge projection TV on two sides.

Jackson toyed with the idea of getting back to work. But sitting here, watching Mallory feed her baby seemed more important at the moment.

"Someone named Nicole. She says to tell you congratulations on your baby and that she's crazy about her new house. You sold it to her?"

Mallory smiled, remembering. "At her wedding. Fastest sale I ever made." Though she was unaware of it, pride filled her voice. "I showed it to her and her fiancé the day before the wedding." She rocked Joshua slightly as he sucked on his bottle. "The next day, they wanted to make an offer on it. The house was vacant and the owners were so happy to sell, they were willing to agree to practically anything. They did away with the standard waiting period before closing escrow." Retracting the nipple for a moment and wiping Joshua's mouth, Mallory did a quick mental calculation. "They should be all moved in by now."

Joshua was eating faster than a hungry shrew, Jackson observed. The bottle was almost empty. "That would explain the invitation."

"Invitation?" She set the bottle down on the coffee table.

Jackson offered her a folded diaper. Taking it, Mallory laid it over her shoulder before positioning Joshua there. "She said to look for one in the mail."

A party. The idea pleased her. She smiled as she patted Joshua's back, coaxing out a burp. "Oh, an open house."

A teasing gleam entered his eyes. "You mean like the one where we—"

"No, not like that one." She cut him off quickly, not wanting Jackson to get started. She was having enough trouble distancing herself from him as it was without taking a stroll down memory lane. "As in new owners having a housewarming party."

A movement outside the window caught his eye. The blue-and-white mail truck was just pulling away from the curb. He rose.

"Mail's here." Jackson crossed to the front door. "I'll get it for you."

He was being too obliging again, she thought. "Don't you have any research to do?"

"Even researchers get to take a break," he said over his shoulder.

He returned in a couple of minutes carrying a sheaf of letters in his hand.

"Look like bills," he announced, flipping through them. "And maybe an invitation." Holding it up, he waved the small envelope at her.

She pulled it out of his hand. "Do you mind? I can look through my own mail." She wanted him out of her mailbox and out of her life. Before she didn't have the strength to send him away.

He surrendered the rest of the mail. "Why doesn't Steven ever write to you? Or is he illiterate as well as Amish?"

Jackson saw the angry spark enter her eyes. It only egged him on. He wanted her to give up this charade, or give him some real proof of the man's existence.

He held up a hand. "No, wait, that's right, you said he went to college, so I guess that rules out illiteracy. That means he's just lazy or doesn't care." He leaned forward, his eyes fixed on hers. "Or don't they have mail where he is, either?"

She had just about enough. "I don't have to justify my relationship with Steven to you, Jackson. I don't have to justify anything at all." Her eyes cut small holes into him. "Now if you can't stay out of my business, you're going to have to leave."

Jackson lifted his hands in mock surrender. "Sorry, lost my head. I'll be good." He could almost see the sarcastic retort forming in her mind. "Really."

The word glided along her skin, a promise of things to come. If he was going to be good, then James Dean had been a choir boy.

She blew out a breath and looked at the mail he'd handed her. Dropping the envelopes on the coffee table, she sorted through them. Mallory decided to open the invitation first. Bills could always be dealt with.

Inside the envelope was a cheerful white card with a cartoon robin very obviously involved in feathering a brand-new nest. The bird proclaimed that the recipient of the card was invited to a housewarming.

"Mothers and babies invited, husbands optional," was handwritten inside, then stated the date and time for the party. It was followed by a hand-written command in big, block letters: COME.

She could do with a party, Mallory thought. Getting out among people again for a few hours would do her good. Joshua gurgled, bringing her around. Mallory looked up and realized that Jackson was reading the invitation over her shoulder. She flipped the card closed.

"How about friends?" Jackson asked, leaning over the back of the sofa. "Are friends optional?"

She shifted around to look at him. He was too close, she thought. Always too close. Doggedly, she dug in. "You're asking if you can come along?"

"Yes." The smile was far too wide to be innocent. He was up to something.

"Why?"

He made himself comfortable on the sofa before answering. "Because I'd like to go to a party with you, meet your friends." Very slowly, he ran the tip of his finger along the rim of her collar. "The last time around, we kind of shut everyone else out."

Yes, she thought, they had. They'd created a world of their own. Which was why it had been so empty for her when he left. There'd been no one left in the world but her. Until she found out about Joshua.

"Stop that." She swatted away his hand.

"As luck would have it," he continued, unfazed, "I'm free on Saturday. And since we can bring Joshua, we won't have to worry about interviewing baby-sitters from now until doomsday."

He was steam rolling right over her. Determined, Mallory stuck to her guns. "What if I don't want you to come?"

That wasn't an option. He was going to get so firmly entrenched in her life before Steven returned that she wasn't going to know where she ended and he began.

"Sure you do," he told her, brushing a casual kiss over her lips. "Now if I'm going to go, I have work to do. I can't stand around here, talking to you all day, you know." He maintained a straight face, though there was humor in his eyes. "No matter how inviting that might be," he added softly.

She sat looking after him as the front door opened and closed. He'd left, his portable computer securely nestled within his traveling bag, to do some research at the college library.

He was crazy. Absolutely crazy.

The problem, she thought as she got up, was that she hadn't had her shots against "crazy." Which was why he was so damn appealing.

But he'd been that way the first time, she reminded herself as she went to call Nicole to confirm the invitation. "And we all remember how that went," she said aloud to Joshua.

Joshua stared at her with Jackson's eyes and Jackson's mouth.

"Oh God," she moaned, shaking her head. She knew she should have kicked Jackson out the moment he'd appeared at the real estate office.

# Ten

Mallory carried Joshua in her arms, leaving Jackson to cope with both the infant seat and the housewarming present as they walked the long block toward Nicole and Dennis's new home. Cars lined the cul-de-sac on both sides, spilling out onto the long through street where Jackson had finally managed to find a spot.

"What have you got in here?" He shifted the infant seat so that the gift couldn't fall out. The concentrated weight felt heavier with each step. "Lead weights?"

"Bookends." Mallory looked over her shoulder at him, a smile playing on her lips as she stopped before the door.

"Cast iron?" Coming up beside her, he exhaled dramatically.

"Stone. Gothic stone." She pulled her hair away from Joshua's grasping fingers. "It's Apollo and Diana. They're heavy because I wanted them to be able to hold really heavy books in place."

He didn't bother asking why. He figured it was a woman

thing she'd only be annoyed at him for not understanding. "I'm sure they'll love it."

She barely touched the doorbell before the front door swung open. A small, lively looking woman with incredibly blue eyes stood in the doorway. The next moment, she was embracing both Mallory and her son in a warm, if careful, hug.

Instantly, Nicole's eyes shifted to the man beside Mallory, appraising him with no small amount of interest. "I was afraid you wouldn't come," Nicole told Mallory. She gestured them inside and closed the door.

Mallory turned to face Nicole, amusement playing on her lips. "I said I would."

Nicole knew how quickly promises could be forgotten, especially in the rush of overly hectic days and sleepless nights.

"Yes, but it is just a few weeks after your delivery." Deftly, she accepted the gaily wrapped package that Jackson offered her. Instantly, she sagged beneath the weight. She looked from Jackson to Mallory. "Wow, what's in here?"

"Near as I can figure, cannonballs." Jackson grinned easily. "Hi, I'm Jackson Cain." He nodded toward Mallory and Joshua. "I'm with them."

If Nicole's smile had been any wider, Mallory was certain it would have split her face. The next moment, the indigo eyes washed over her in closer scrutiny. "Are you sure you should be out and around? I know I bullied you into coming, but if you didn't feel up to it—"

Mallory waved away Nicole's concern. She purposely didn't glance at Jackson's face, knowing that she would only see a smug look there. They both knew just how fit she felt.

"What, you think you and your sister have a patent on recuperating quickly? If this was the old days, I'd be back in the fields, working two hours after I'd had the baby."

Though she was standing just shy of the doorway, Mallory could see into the crowded living room. Everything had been repainted, refitted, or repapered. In an incredibly short amount of time, Nicole had taken ten years worth of living by the previous owners and erased it, turning the house into something that was brand-new. Instead of the old, French provincial furniture that the past owner had insisted on maintaining, Nicole had brought in wide, comfortable pieces that called to the beholder to sit and be comfortable. To put his feet up.

Imprisoned by dark colors, the room had been tight and small looking when Mallory had shown it. Now, even crowded with guests, it had a spacious, airy look. The heavy, navy drapes were gone, replaced by pastel vertical blinds that stood at the ends of the various rods like lean sentries waiting to be deployed.

Talk about a makeover.

"Wow, I really love what you've done with the place, Nicole."

It hadn't been easy doing it all on a self-imposed budget, but Nicole refused to tap into her trust fund any more than was absolutely necessary. She wanted to do this on her own. Their own, she amended, thinking of Dennis.

Proud of her efforts, Nicole beamed. "I'm not nearly done yet."

Coming up behind her to greet the new arrivals, her husband groaned. "She means that," Dennis interjected, pretending to be taxed. It was no secret that he was pleased with what Nicole had accomplished. Coordination for him didn't go beyond not mixing stripes with polka dots, but he could appreciate the results as well as anyone. "Me, I like things simple."

Nicole leaned toward Mallory and Jackson and said in a stage whisper, "Translated, orange crates strategically centered around a TV set."

Dennis saw no reason to disagree. "Hey, orange crates are easier to move around when she gets the bug to have the furniture go square dancing." He looked at Jackson, confident that he had found a commiserating soul mate. They looked like a couple, Dennis judged. "And she gets it a lot," he confided. Dennis turned toward Mallory. "Check your baby for you?"

She blinked. "Excuse me?"

Looking for Nicole, Marlene Bailey Travis came to join the small circle in the foyer. As blond as her younger sister was dark, it was only when Marlene smiled that the family resemblance was evident. That and the fact that both women had eyes the color of a lagoon at sunset.

"Hello," she extended her hand to Jackson. "I think we met in the real estate office the day Mallory went into labor. I'm Marlene. The warmee's sister." She nodded at Nicole. "And what my brother-in-law is trying to say is that we seem to be running a regular day care here."

Marlene's heart swelled as she looked down at Mallory's son. Robby was a little more than three months old now, taking on a personality of his own. He seemed so much bigger than the infant in Mallory's arms. After seeing her niece and nephew, as well as Erin's son, Jamie, Marlene decided that she was completely hooked on the sight and powdery scent of babies. With any luck at all, by this time next year, Robby would have a sibling to bully.

"Sally's in the guest bedroom, holding down the fort," she explained.

"Sally?" Jackson was attempting to process names as quickly as they came in. As he scanned the large room just beyond the foyer, he didn't see people so much as characters with which to flesh out the pages of his new book.

"My housekeeper," Marlene told him. For his benefit, she elaborated further. "Actually, she was more like a nanny to us. She practically raised Nicole and me and she absolutely refused to stay home with her feet up tonight when Sullivan and I left for the party with Robby." A fond smile curved her mouth. "I honestly think that she doesn't believe I can take care of Robby on my own."

A tall, dark-haired man strolled into their midst. He laid a proprietary hand on Marlene's shoulder. The gesture instantly identified his role in the play for Jackson. "That's because she doesn't know just how capable you are. Hello." He smiled at Mallory and her baby and shook Jackson's hand. "I'm Sullivan Travis, Marlene's husband."

"Jackson Cain," Jackson replied. "Mallory's... friend," he added significantly, his eyes touching Mallory's. He noticed the color creeping up along her neck and wondered at its source.

"Oh, she knows, all right," Nicole corrected her brother-in-law. "Sally just refuses to admit the fact that we've long since passed needing her to supervise every detail in our lives."

Marlene laughed, teasing her sister. "That's because you were such a hellion when you were growing up. She's afraid you'll drop one of the twins."

Tit for tat. "Then how do you explain her hovering over you?" Nicole countered.

Seeing his wife and sister-in-law on the verge of a lengthy discussion that would delve far into the past, Dennis exchanged looks with Sullivan. Each man began to usher his wife toward the living room.

"Why don't we all get out of the foyer and into the rest of the house?" Dennis suggested. "Before we start impeding traffic."

"Terrific idea," Marlene agreed. Disengaging herself from Sullivan, she took Mallory's arm. "It looks as if we have some catching up to do." Her eyes shifted toward Jackson.

"Jackson's just an old friend," Mallory said hastily. "Like he said."

Dennis caught the slight hesitation in Mallory's voice. It was hard to turn the instincts he'd honed on his job off, even when he wasn't working. As a law enforcement agent for the Treasury Department, he was more aware than most other people that things were usually not exactly what they seemed. There was a story here. He'd leave it to his wife to uncover it. He'd find out soon enough.

"Well, 'old friend'," he said easily. "How about a drink?"

"Sounds great," Jackson readily agreed.

Nicole handed the housewarming gift to Dennis. She couldn't wait to get Mallory away from Jackson and start asking questions. "Here, put this with the other gifts, will you, honey?"

Dennis obliged, then lifted a brow as he felt the solid weight in his hands. "Bookends," Jackson explained.

"I'll be sure to keep them out of Nicole's reach." Dennis firmly believed in prevention. He'd seen her temper erupt only once, but that was once too much. It was always better to be safe, than sorry.

Marlene had waited long enough. "Let me hold him," she coaxed Mallory. "Come here, precious," she cooed as Mallory surrendered Joshua to her.

Sullivan watched the glow on Marlene's face as his wife led the way to the ground floor guest room. "I think we're going to be in for a very large family in the not too distant future." He turned to the other two men. "Marlene looks as if she has the nesting instinct every time she gets near a baby. One isn't going to be enough for her. She's already moaning that Robby is growing up too fast."

Jackson could see that the idea of having more children didn't only please Marlene, but Sullivan as well. He was beginning to understand where they were coming from.

Mallory looked uncertainly over her shoulder at Jackson. She was leaving him in a room full of people he didn't know. "You'll be all right?"

"He'll be fine," Dennis assured her. "You'd better go along with Nicole before she bursts." He nodded at his wife. "Don't put her on the torture rack unless she absolutely refuses to crack," he instructed Nicole.

Nicole gave him an impudent look that she couldn't quite manage to carry off, then turned to Mallory. Moving her along, she got about ten feet away before she finally squealed, "So? What's up?"

"Interest rates on mortgages." Somehow, Mallory managed to keep a straight face. "You and Dennis got in just in time."

Marlene was more subdued than her sister, but no less curious. "You know what she means," she prodded. "He's very handsome. Who is he?"

"Handsome? The man is drop-dead gorgeous," Erin Lockwood cried as she came up behind Mallory. "If I didn't have Brady, I'd be willing to wrestle you to the ground for him. Best two throws out of three."

Her green eyes glimmered as she quickly kissed Mallory's cheek. She and Mallory had gotten to know one another, as well as Nicole and Marlene, while sitting in Sheila Pollack's reception area, waiting for their turns on the examining table. Solidly connected by their pregnancies and by the fact that each had faced the prospect of raising a child alone at the outset, the four women had shared each other's sorrows to a greater or lesser extent as well as each other's joys.

Now, it seemed, was the time for sharing joy. That would be the heading she'd put the man under, Erin thought, glancing in his direction again. Pure joy.

"Your baby's beautiful," Erin declared.

Touching the tiny fist, she found her finger immediately swallowed up by a questing hand. The next moment, Joshua brought his new prize to his mouth. Erin laughed, extracting her finger.

"And hungry. Perpetually hungry," Mallory sighed. She patted her shoulder bag, filled to capacity with supplies to face any emergency three times over. "I'd better go and feed him."

"Sally can do that for you," Nicole told her.

She wanted Mallory to relax. If it hadn't been for Mallory, she, Dennis and the twins would undoubtedly still be living in the small garden apartment where she had lived before she married Dennis. His studio apartment had been too small to house them and even the apartment had been crammed, what with two babies and a lumbering dog with the improbable name of Romeo constantly underfoot.

Mallory looked at Nicole doubtfully. "Won't she mind?"

"Mind?" Marlene echoed with a soft laugh. "Since the babies have entered her life, Sally's like a young woman again. A young woman who works as a drill sergeant in the army, but a young woman nonetheless," she added fondly. "Trust me, she'll fight you for the right to feed and change him."

"C'mon," Nicole urged, "let's go tend to your son."

"And then you tell us all about Mr. Drop-dead Gorgeous," Erin put in.

Marlene glanced back toward Jackson. He was buffered on either side by her husband and her brother-in-law. She saw Erin's husband, Brady, joining the men and smiled to herself. It made for a nice group photo, she thought. Ever the hostess, even at her sister's house, Marlene was pleased that the men were getting along so well.

She noted Jackson's profile as he turned toward Sullivan. Something Mallory had said to her about a brooding artist rang a bell. She looked down at Joshua. The baby had the same raven black hair.

Her eyes met Mallory's. "Jackson is Joshua's father, isn't he?" she asked softly.

The other two women were silent, waiting for Mallory's answer.

Mallory looked at Marlene sharply, then her eyes shifted over toward Jackson.

*I knew it,* Marlene thought. "Don't worry," Marlene assured Mallory gently. Jackson was standing with his back turned toward them. "He couldn't have possibly heard me. And even if he reads lips, I doubt if he can do it with the back of his head."

"His father?" Nicole echoed when Mallory made no reply one way or the other.

"Really?" Erin breathed.

Not one to hold back, the short, auburn-haired woman threw her arms around Mallory and squeezed hard in silent camaraderie. She'd only recently been reunited with her own husband, but that had been because Brady had been mugged late one night, leaving her house. The resulting amnesia had kept him away from her for five months. It could have been forever. Erin knew the incredible joy of reunion.

Releasing Mallory, she blinked back tears of sympathy. "Oh, how wonderful."

She wished it were as simple as that. "Not so wonderful," Mallory commented.

Instantly, Nicole interpreted her words. "He doesn't know?"

Mallory shook her head.

Stunned at the revelation, Erin couldn't think of a single reason for not telling Jackson that he was Joshua's father. "Why not?"

Mallory sighed, wondering if the reasons would sound trite to them. But they were so very important to her. "I don't want him staying because he has to." *And if he doesn't stay, it'll break my heart.*

Marlene considered herself a fair judge of character. She had seen the way Jackson had looked at Mallory when he had introduced himself. A blind man could see that there was something between them. And that Jackson wanted it that way.

"He doesn't look like a man who's staying because he has to," she observed.

She wasn't going to be talked into it, not even by her friends. She knew Jackson better than anyone. "That's because he's free right now. Free to come and go." Mallory leaned over and pressed a kiss to her son's head, remembering. "And most likely, he will."

Marlene heard the pain in Mallory's voice and her heart ached for her friend. Loving someone was never an easy business; it shouldn't be made more complicated than it already was.

"Don't you think you owe it to him to make the choice?" Marlene asked her.

The door behind them opened. A short, squat woman with iron gray hair stood in the doorway, looking like a wizen troll at the gates of fairyland.

"Don't let a man have a choice," Sally snapped. Without an introduction or any acknowledgment to the newest arrival, Sally took the baby from Marlene's hands. "Make it for him and let him think it's his." She gave her head a final nod. "Only way to deal with 'em."

Marlene threaded her arm around the thin shoulders. She'd leaned her head on them countless times as a child. "We come to Sally with all our lovelorn problems," Marlene told Mallory with a wink.

"And then do just the opposite," Nicole concluded. As Sally bristled loudly, Nicole kissed her wrinkled cheek, not paying any attention. It was a game of long standing. Their mutual affection went without saying. "Sally, this is Mallory Flannigan. She sold me the house. Sold us the house," Nicole amended.

God, it was still all so new to her. It was difficult to think of herself as a married woman again.

Or perhaps for the first time, Nicole corrected herself, looking over her shoulder toward Dennis. Her first marriage, done in haste to escape the long reach of an unloving father, didn't count. Nothing counted until Dennis had appeared. Because everything with Dennis was brand-new.

Begun in a lie, their relationship had been purified and refined until it was something precious, something, she was certain, no one else had ever experienced.

Although, she glanced at the circle of women around her, she was willing to concede that some probably came close.

"All right, now get out." Holding Joshua against her in one arm, Sally waved the women toward the party with her other hand. "You're all underfoot," Sally scowled. "And remember to keep that slobbering mutt out of here." Something that passed for a smile appeared on her thin lips.

"I'm talking about the dog," she said pointedly, "Not any of the guests."

Marlene and Nicole merely exchanged looks and shook their heads. There would never be any changing Sally. And it was probably for the best.

"Joshua's hungry," Mallory began to protest as the others started to usher her away. She handed over her shoulder bag.

Sally let the purse drop on the floor inside the door. "I figured that out on my own." She looked at Mallory expectantly, waiting for her to leave. "Well? Do I look feeble? Do I look as if I can't hold a bottle to a baby's lips?"

Mallory relented and began to relax. "No, ma'am." She grinned.

"Then get out." Sally pointed to the party. "Have a good time." Pale blue eyes looked from one woman to the other. "They'll all be here when you're finished." With that, Sally firmly closed the door on them.

Mallory fervently wished there had been a Sally in her life, or someone who would have even come close. When she'd been alive, her own mother had been far more interested in herself than in raising a daughter. And her father had long since disappeared from the scene without a single trace. She hadn't seen him since she was eight.

It was nice to have someone to care about you, she thought, glancing toward the closed door. "She's quite the martinet, isn't she?" Because it was her house, Mallory directed her question to Nicole.

Nicole nodded. "That she is. And this is mellow compared to the way she used to be."

She and Sally had butted heads more than once when Nicole was growing up. Denied a mother's love for reasons she only recently had been made aware of, chafing against a father whose only family was work, Nicole had been hell-bent on grabbing life by the ears and shaking it, demanding to know why she had gotten a short stick. Neither Marlene nor Sally ever gave up on her. She was grateful to both.

"And I wouldn't trade her in for a dozen nannies," Marlene acknowledged firmly. "C'mon," she threaded her arm through Mallory's "she's right, you know. Let's join the party."

Mallory willingly allowed herself to be led away. She needed to laugh.

"I like them." Jackson handed Mallory a glass of punch. He'd given her some space, letting her mingle with her friends for a while before joining her. He'd learned a few things in the process.

The glass was frosty. Mallory hadn't realized she was warm until the cool feel of the surface against her fingers registered. She drank gratefully, then looked at Jackson. "Who?"

"Your friends." He nodded toward Marlene and Nicole who had joined their husbands on the patio. Erin and Brady were in the doorway by the kitchen, oblivious to the fact that anyone else was around. "Did you know that Dennis was a law enforcement agent for the Treasury Department?"

Jackson watched as Dennis nuzzled Nicole, whispering something in her ear. She laughed and kissed him.

He wanted that sort of easy romance, Jackson thought with envy. He wanted to feel that comfortable with someone, to have them end his sentences and share his feelings. His eyes shifted to Mallory.

"I thought I could get together with him sometime and ask him a few questions for my book." There were technical details that he needed to iron out before continuing with the novel.

Mallory nodded, taking in the information. Watching Nicole and Dennis standing as close as she was to Jackson hurt. It only made her think of what she ultimately couldn't have. A marriage with someone who could be an equal partner, not someone who was versed in disappearing acts.

"Then I guess this wasn't a total loss for you."

He looked at her. What an odd way to put it. "Loss? What are you talking about?"

She nodded as she took another sip. The punch wasn't cold enough anymore. "Coming here with me. I thought you'd be bored."

The corners of his mouth rose. How could he ever be bored as long as she was around? "No, I'm not bored. I am curious, however."

"About what?"

"Well, these are all your friends, right?" He began slowly.

"Some of them," she acknowledged. There was something in his tone she didn't care for. Instantly, she was on her guard. "Why?"

"Well, if they're your friends, why hasn't anyone asked you about Steven?" Neither Dennis, Sullivan nor Brady had known anything about the man and Jackson was certain that one of their wives would have mentioned Steven in passing. If he existed.

She shrugged casually, her insides tightening into a knot. "They never met him. Steven tends to be shy around strangers."

Jackson nodded sagely, pretending to take it all in. "Ah yes, the Amish in him."

Mallory turned on him. The look in her eyes was accusing. She wasn't going to cause a scene, but she didn't want to listen to this, either. "Don't spoil this afternoon for me, Jackson."

"How? By talking about Steven?" He saw the hurt look in her eyes and smoothed over the edge in his voice. "I'm not spoiling, Mallory, I'm digging. It's the writer in me," he explained. "I like knowing things." Very easily, he slipped his arm around her. "I wanted to find out some more things about my competition so I could blow him out of the water."

She raised her head and met the look in his eyes. *Why can't I look into your soul, Jackson? Is it because you don't have one? How can I possibly ever believe you again?* "And then what?"

He touched her cheek. God, but he wanted her. Here, surrounded with a room full of people, he couldn't think of anything else but peeling the dress away from her and feasting on her body. Kissing every inch of her satiny skin until she was a mindless puddle in his hands, to do with what he would. And what he would do, he realized, was worship.

And then make love with her until they both expired. "And then occupy the waters where he'd been," he told her euphemistically.

"Why?" she pressed.

His hand cupping her chin, he rubbed his thumb along her bottom lip. Desire blossomed in her eyes, full-bodied like a cactus flower blooming overnight. "Why do you think?"

"I think," she answered haltingly, trying not to let him affect her, "you might not want something, but you hate the idea of someone else having it."

He dropped his hand, staring at her. "Is that what you really think?"

Mallory looked away, afraid to think anything else. Wanting so desperately to believe otherwise. "I don't know."

Jackson nodded slowly. He supposed he couldn't fault her, not at bottom. He'd done this to himself, she hadn't.

"Well then, think about it. And take your time, Mallory," he counseled quietly. "Take all the time you need. As long as you come to the right conclusion."

"And what is the right conclusion?" *Please, somehow, I have to know.*

He smiled into her eyes. There was love there somewhere, he thought. And so, there was hope. "You'll know it when you get there. It'll seem right. *Feel* right. Be right." He whispered the last words into her ear, a prophesy.

Setting down his glass on the end table, Jackson looked at her. Then, unmindful of the others around him, he brought his mouth down to hers.

"Just like that," he promised.

If only she could believe him. Mallory wedged her hands between them, swallowing and trying to clear her throat.

"I think I had better go check on the baby."

"I'll come with you," he offered.

"No," she said very firmly, "You won't come with me."

*But I will,* Jackson thought as he watched her walk away through the crowded room. *Make no mistake about it, Mallory. Someday, I will.*

# Eleven

Mallory leaned her chin on the side of the headrest in the car. Behind her, Joshua was sound asleep in his infant seat. She sighed as she looked at him. Light and dark shadows played across him, like a hand lightly stroking his face. "Sometimes I still can't believe he's really here."

Jackson laughed quietly. "I would have thought that the labor pains would have left an indelible mark on your memory."

Jackson spared her a smile as he guided the car down MacArthur Boulevard. Twilight had dyed everything in its path an inky black. In the distance, the lights from residential homes dotted the hillside terrain like a thousand fireflies frozen in midflight.

"No, not really." Satisfied that Joshua would continue sleeping peacefully, she turned around in her seat and faced forward. "It's true what they say."

Well, that came out of nowhere. "And what is it that they say?"

"That you forget about the pain once you hold your baby in your arms." Mallory slanted a look at Jackson. She'd been looking for an opening all night. Questions were straining to break free, especially one in particular.

"Does forgetting pertain to only your own tiny baby, or to all babies in general?" A smile curved his mouth as he elaborated. "As in 'Baby, It's Cold Outside,' or another endearment?" Was she trying to say that what had happened between them earlier was forgiven, or was he reading far too much into her words?

"*My* baby," she clarified.

Mallory stared straight ahead as a love song wafted over the radio. Something he had said the other day had been gnawing at her. Now was as good a time as any to ask. Knowing the answer would pave the way to other things for her that finally had to be said.

"Botched as in how?"

"What?" He turned to look at Mallory as he eased his foot onto the brake. A few feet away, the traffic light gleamed like a suspended glittering ruby.

In the few months they had been together, she had only managed to put together a sketchy background on Jackson. She knew he had a trust fund left to him by his grandfather and that he didn't care for his family. Beyond that, he hadn't elaborated. He had been interested in the here and now, rather than what had gone before. Suddenly, it was important that she know more about the father of her child.

"You said your parents botched up your childhood, or words to that effect." Her eyes met his in the dim light from the street lamps that bowed their heads along both sides of the lonely road. "Exactly what did you mean by that?"

Jackson shrugged, pressing down on the accelerator. The light was green. "Slip of the tongue."

She was familiar with that tone. It signaled the closing of a door. Mallory stared at his profile. Was it her imagination, or had it hardened? "So you don't want to talk about it."

He rarely thought of Alexis and Walter Cain as his parents anymore. They were just two people who happened to bear the same name as he did, nothing more. "Not particularly."

She should have known better. Mallory sighed. "You know, I was almost beginning to believe you were serious about changing." That would teach her. Nothing had changed. Nothing would ever change between them. Why couldn't she just accept that and be done with it? "But you're still playing games, still keeping the door closed on your life."

"Maybe it's because it's not a pretty life, despite the money."

The lights seemed to be with them now. They'd be home soon. Jackson blew out a breath, making a decision. He glanced at Mallory as he drove down the last leg of the trip.

"You really want to know?"

Jackson made it sound as if it were some sort of initiation rite she'd be better off avoiding if at all possible. But she didn't want to avoid it. She wanted to know. "Yes."

"All right, I'll tell you." Mallory watched his face as he spoke. There was a casual disinterest in his voice, but his jaw was rigid. "My parents had what you might call an arranged marriage. His money, her money, it sounded good to them at the time and they were a 'handsome couple' I think the term is." There was no denying that they looked good together on the society page, but the posed photographs never captured what really existed beneath the expensive clothing.

A touch of sarcasm entered his voice, hardening it. "The only problem these handsome people had was that they didn't love each other."

He remembered the frosty arguments. The snide remarks. "Or the son they created to carry on the name." There had been no love, no warmth, only expectations. Expectations he quickly learned to thwart. "My grandfather liked me a lot better than my father did." Though a hard man to get to know, there were times when Jackson believed that his grandfather was his only friend.

Robert Livingston Cain was not without his faults, but to a lonely little boy, he represented the only source of approval Jackson had.

He smiled fondly now, a collage of words and scenes passing through his mind. "He was crusty, but he had his moments. The only thing my father and grandfather had in common, besides their surname, was a love of women." There was one in particular, a high-priced call girl named Annette. His grandfather had offered him a night with her as a gift for his fifteenth birthday.

"High time we got you initiated, Jack." He'd eyed his grandson, tugging at his white handlebar mustache thoughtfully. "Time you knew how to put that equipment the good Lord issued you to some use."

It had turned out to be one hell of a birthday, Jackson thought.

"Grandpa did have an eye for the ladies, but at least he made sure Grandma didn't know. Dad wasn't so discreet." He supposed that was what separated the two generations. Polite hypocrisy. His voice was flat, devoid of emotion as he continued. "Mother tried to kill herself three times, never quite successfully."

Jackson remembered the terror he felt the first time. All of ten, he'd been the one to discover Alexis, sprawled out in her king-size bed, an empty bottle of sleeping pills lying beside her, a dramatically worded suicide note on the floor. He'd been hysterical, calling for help, begging her not to die. When she'd recovered, she'd chastised him for entering her room uninvited. He did a lot of growing that year.

"I think she engineered the suicide attempts just to get back at him." Even he knew better by the time he was eleven. "As if my father would have cared."

Mallory shivered, imagining how he must have felt. She knew what it was like not to have either parent's love. Instantly, her heart went out to him.

"And where were you during all this?" she asked in a soft whisper.

"Boarding schools, mostly." He'd been sent away after that first attempt. Neither parent had wanted him underfoot. "A lot of them," he added. He glanced at her as he pulled up into her driveway. "In case you haven't noticed, I don't do authority too well."

Mallory's mouth curved with affection. "Yes, I noticed."

He pulled up the hand brake. Those had been his formative years, he supposed. They had taught him how to get along on his own. Taught him that he didn't really need anyone to depend on, except himself. Made him afraid to depend on anyone, he realized now.

"I got kicked out of a lot of schools." The notoriety had really irked his father, which was why he had continued rebelling. "My father threatened to cut me off. My grandfather overruled him. Grandpa had control of the money, actually."

Jackson supposed that irritated Walter most of all. Walter had wanted to have the old man declared incompetent and take over the family fortune, but Robert Livingston Cain had a battery of lawyers who were unbeatable and, Walter found, unbribable.

"There was some vicious name calling. The upshot of it was I left home, a tidy trust fund at my disposal whenever I needed it." He wasn't ashamed of having money. It made life easier for him. Not easy, just easier. If he couldn't have their love, at least he could have the comfort their money could provide.

Maybe it was the light from the street lamp, but he could have sworn he saw tears shimmering in her eyes when he looked at Mallory. He didn't want pity. All that had happened a long time ago, in another lifetime. Maybe even to another boy. He'd grown beyond it and he'd put it way behind him.

"Don't look so bleak, it gave me a lot of fodder for stories." He'd told her this much, he might as well say the rest. "Just not a very good handle on how to make a relationship work." God knew he didn't have anything to emulate. "Maybe that's why I'm so bad at it."

She would have been the first to say it, but now that he had, all Mallory wanted to do was comfort him. "Not so bad, really." Impulsively, she kissed his cheek.

He could feel love radiating from her. Damn, but she had managed to burrow her way into his life, clear down to the core.

"Why, Mallory, I do believe you're being nice."

Jackson leaned over and unbuckled her seat belt for her, easing the shoulder strap away from her body. his knuckles just barely brushed along her breasts. He felt rather than heard her sharp intake of breath.

"Did I ever tell you that I'm a sucker for nice?" Jackson glanced at the infant seat strapped down in the back and its dozing occupant. His eyes shifted toward Mallory's. "Think he'll stay that way for a while?"

She knew exactly what he was asking. And exactly what she wanted. "We can hope."

He smiled. Hope. He liked the sound of that word. Liked it in connection with her. It wasn't one that turned up in his life very often.

"Yes," Jackson agreed, running the back of his hand along her cheek slowly, exciting them both, "we can always hope."

Mallory eased out of the nursery, partially closing the door behind her. So far, so good, she thought.

As she walked downstairs again, she held her hair up, away from her neck. The day had been an unseasonably warm one. The encroaching night hadn't managed to bring any cooler weather with it.

Jackson was reclining on the sofa, a yellow ruled pad resting on his outstretched legs. He was writing in furious snatches.

The creative process at work, she mused, wondering what he was writing. He seemed oblivious to everything else around him. Mallory began to withdraw.

Feeling her presence, Jackson looked up. He raised a brow, waiting.

"He's still asleep." No longer hot, she let her hair drop. Rather than warmth, a chill was claiming her.

Why else did she feel like trembling?

Because she was unsure, that's why, Mallory told herself. *It has to be done.*

Mallory crossed to the coffee table and perched on the edge, facing him. This wasn't going to be easy. What would he say when he found out? When he learned that she had not only kept this from him, but actively lied in order to keep it a secret?

"I'm beginning to think I should try to steal Sally away from Marlene. Whatever she did with Joshua seems to have worked."

The baby had woken up when she had changed him, but then fell asleep again, as if he had spent the afternoon partying the way they had.

Mallory bit her lip. She was chattering, she thought uncomfortably. Battling nerves, Marlene's voice was still ringing in her ears, urging her to tell Jackson that Joshua was his.

It was the only right thing to do. During the course of the afternoon and ensuing evening, watching Jackson interact with her friends, and now, listening to his story, Mallory had felt progressively guiltier and guiltier for having withheld the truth. A man had the right to know that he had a son.

But what of the son's rights?

The question gnawed at her the way it had over the last few days. Torn, Mallory made up her mind. "Jackson, maybe we do need to talk."

The pad slid from his lap as he sat up. *Oh-oh.* Forestalling something he felt he might not care to hear, Jackson took her hands in his.

"Later," he told Mallory softly. "We can talk later."

Right now, all he wanted to do was make love with her. If he was honest with himself, that was all he had really thought about all afternoon. All evening. Making torturously slow, sensual love with her over and over again until neither of them had the strength to stand up, much less walk.

No. The single word beat urgently in her head. This had to be gotten out in the open now, before she lost her nerve. Before she changed her mind again.

"But—." Her lips parted haltingly in protest.

It was all the invitation Jackson needed. In a fluid motion, he slid from the sofa to kneel in front of her. At the same time, his mouth gently took possession of hers.

He felt her sigh against his lips, whether in surrender or resignation, he didn't know. It didn't matter. What mattered was that the taste of her excited him and that she was here with him tonight.

Slowly, Jackson moved his mouth over hers, making love to her with only his lips and his tongue. Powerful weapons in the right hands.

Mallory moaned, her mind swimming, already in danger of being lost. "No, really." No matter how much she tried, she couldn't force herself to pull more than an inch away from him. "I have to tell you…"

She was going to tell him to stop, worse, to leave. He couldn't bear to hear it, not while he wanted her this way. He had to make her change her mind before the words were spoken.

"Later," he promised. "I'll listen to anything you have to say later. But right now," his breath caressed her face, "I'm on a mission of mercy. A quest for mercy, really."

"Mercy?" If there was any, she wouldn't feel completely boneless now. She'd be able to think of something other than making love with him.

"Yes, I've been aching for you all day. If you have any mercy, you'll take pity on me. 'That I shall die is true, but for my love.'"

When he set his mind to it, he could probably charm a bear right out of wanting to hibernate. Mallory laughed, shaking her head. "You don't have to quote poetry to make love with me, Jackson."

Still on his knees, his fingers played along her shoulders. The loose blouse easily slid down, pooling like green mist about her waist. He raised his eyes to hers. "What do I have to do?"

She felt his fingers undoing the clasp at her back with only a flick of his fingers. The shiver that came to claim her arrived for a different reason than the one before it. Hypnotized, she watched his eyes as he slid the bra straps from her arms.

"Just be, Jackson. Just be."

Rising, he brought her up with him, gathering her in his arms. "I intend to." Unable to resist, he pressed a kiss to her throat, his hands claiming her breasts, branding them with familiar heat. "I want to grow old with you, Mallory. I want to be there with you when my teeth fall out and gravity shifts everything southward for both of us." He'd never felt like that about anyone before. And knew that he never would again.

His thumbs were teasing her nipples. It was hard not to move in time to the rhythm of the arousal he was creating. Mallory cupped his face in her hands. Desire drummed impatiently through her, but it took a back seat to the love she felt embracing her.

"Jackson, you do know how to pitch an argument." Whatever she'd been thinking of was gone, flown out of her head to make room for the splashes of color and emotion occupying it now.

It wasn't a pitch. It was a proposal. The most important of his life. Because it didn't have to do with a novel, it had to do with life. His and hers. And Joshua's.

"No punches this time, Mallory," he swore. "I'm pulling no punches. Just the truth."

The truth. Like a thorny rose, it pricked at her. He was offering her his true feelings and she'd been keeping the truth from him all this time.

How would he react, knowing that she'd lied? Lied to him ever since he'd returned?

He saw things in her eyes, indecision, hesitation. Uncertainty. She probably didn't know whether or not to believe him. He intended to wipe all indecision from her mind. He knew he'd turned from her and deserved whatever he got, but in his heart, he hoped, prayed, she wouldn't choose to turn away from him now.

He had to make her forgive him. Now and forever.

For once, things had to be said aloud, not just written about. Caressing her face, he told her the words that were already written in his heart.

"I love you, Mallory. I came back to see you again, hoping the sight of you would cure me." What a fool he'd been. "But seeing you just made the disease that much worse."

Her brows drew together as she tried to understand what he was telling her. "So now I'm a disease?"

"No." Shaking his head in denial, Jackson brought his lips down to her breasts. He felt the sigh shiver out from within her as his mouth skimmed each. "More like a fever. A fever of the blood."

She would have loved to quote something poetic back at him, but her mind was more tangled than skeins of wool in a den of kittens. A small rhyme was all she could manage. "I yearn, therefor I burn?"

He smiled down into her upturned face. She was talking about a physical reaction and he wasn't. Not any longer. "It goes a lot deeper than that, Mallory. A lot deeper."

She had to tell him. As afraid as she was of his reaction for the lie, she had to tell him before this went further. Marlene was right. He had to know. He'd hate her if he found out by accident.

"Jackson—"

He brought his finger to her lips, stilling them. Banishing any words she might be tempted to say.

"No more words, Mallory." He kissed her mouth lightly. "No more words." His breath upon her face, Jackson deepened the kiss, deepened it so that it erased all her words.

And all his own.

There were no more words, no more thoughts, just the passion that reared and bucked within its restraint, the passion they both so desperately wanted to steep themselves in.

Hands hot on her body, he urged her flared skirt away from her waist, down her legs. It joined her blouse in a circle about her feet. She stood dressed in high-heeled sandals, cream panties, and his gaze.

He realized that he'd broken the clasp on her skirt when he'd pulled on it roughly. "I'm going to have to replace that," he murmured against her skin, sending shock waves through her as his lips nipped here, there.

Mallory pulled the last of the buttons out of the hole of his shirt. Fevered, she yanked it off his arms. Her voice was as thick as syrup. As thick as her desire. "With what, Jackson?"

Impatience nearly made him tear off her panties as well. Ridding her of them, he lifted Mallory up to him, hands clasped about her hips. He gave her the only answer he could. "With me."

Mallory twined her legs about his body, cleaving to him like an iron rod to a high-powered magnet, without choice, powerless to do otherwise.

Her mouth sealed to his, her body hot, she dug her fingers into his hair. Mallory covered his face with kisses powered by such an urgency, she almost succeeded in making him roughly take her right where he stood.

But at the last possible moment, as his body primed, he caught himself.

Not now, he couldn't act the beast now, not when he was trying to persuade her that his love of her went beyond the physical, beyond needs that frantically clawed at him to be freed.

He loved her from the depth and breadth of him. Wanting to entrap her, to give her no choice but to love him, he'd only sprung the trap shut further on himself. And now he was more of a helpless prisoner than she. He didn't want her for a night, or a month, or a year. He wanted her forever.

"Whoa, slow down," he begged her. If she didn't, he couldn't.

Jackson caught her face in his hands, stilling her mouth. Her eyes looked dazed, like a woman caught up in a hurricane of the soul.

"Mallory," he pleaded, "I can't hold back if you go on this way."

She didn't want him to hold back, ever. She wanted him to take her roughly, like a barbarian at the door. Pressing her body even closer, she looked into his eyes. "Then don't."

Her words nearly broke the final bands. It was as if he had no will of his own. Where before, he could always walk away, he couldn't anymore. Not with her.

"Oh, woman, what have you done to me? I can't think for wanting you."

He couldn't have said anything worse than if he tried. Mallory stiffened, sliding down until her feet touched the floor. The fire left instantly, as if a bucket of ice cold water had been thrown on her.

Jackson looked at her, stunned. He didn't understand. "What? What did I say?"

He knew what he'd said. What he was telling her. Again. "That I'm interfering in your work again." This was it. He was going to make love with her one more time before he left. Here she was, agonizing over not telling him about his child, and all the while, he was preparing to leave her.

Where had she gotten that from? "No, it's just the opposite. You're Julia." He saw the confusion in her eyes. He was getting ahead of himself. "My heroine." A heroine he'd wound up fashioning after Mallory. Gutsy, exciting and unwilling to let life walk on her. "When I came back, I used research as an excuse." A satisfied smile lifted the corners of his mouth. "But it turns out that I really am working. You're not my hindrance, Mallory." He stroked her hair, his fingers lightly playing with the slope of her throat. "You're my muse. My inspiration."

*My everything.*

She wanted to believe, dear Lord, she wanted to believe. But she was so afraid to. "Then you're not going to leave?"

He shook his head, drawing her closer to him. She had to be made to understand. "I can't leave, Mallory. Not ever. It would be like breaking in half." She was his other half. The best half. She had to believe that. He'd make her believe that.

Mallory raised herself up on her toes to capture his mouth, her breasts lightly trailing along his chest. He shivered with anticipation, his arms firmly closing over her again.

And then, as he had asked, there were no more words. No more anything but just the raw feelings that had been given clearance to enter.

With urgency, she tugged away at the last of his clothing, frustrated fingers trying to unnotch a belt that stubbornly resisted her efforts.

She felt his smile against her mouth as he did the job for her, never braking their connection. She felt the moan born within him transfer to her lips as she hurried the slacks and briefs from his legs down to the floor with her own clothing.

And then they were nude, as nude as on the first day of existence.

Which had begun in each other's arms.

His hands raced along her body, assuring himself that this was real, that it wasn't just wishful thinking on his part. That she'd come to him without hesitancy, without reservations clinging to her like unwashed residue, the way they had the last time.

She was his for the taking. His for the loving.

And he did.

· He loved her with all his heart. Following his fantasy, he trailed his lips along her body, tasting what he already knew, reestablishing claims already filed.

As he slid down to his knees before her a second time, his tongue anointing her between her thighs, Mallory dug her fingers into his hair, wanting to draw him away, wanting to urge him on further.

"Open for me."

The murmured command pierced the haze about her brain. When she did as he instructed, Jackson captured the essence that was her. He drove his tongue in until she sobbed out his name as she scrambled up to one crescent and then hovered above it timelessly.

The ecstasy mounted and flowered until she didn't think she could bear it any longer.

"Jackson." His name came out on a muffled cry, echoing in her head. "Stop, I can't—I can't—" She couldn't even finish the sentence, the thought.

She didn't have to. His lips were on hers, his body eager to take what his mouth had primed.

"Yes, you can." The husky voice murmured along her throat. "We both can." Arms around her, he brought her down to the sofa. She felt the smooth material against her back, against her buttocks.

She was falling back on a cloud. And he was there with her.

*Please, now,* she thought in desperation. She needed him to take her now. She didn't want to scale another summit on her own. Not without him.

And still he teased her, still he held back from the final thrust that would free them both. And imprison them both.

Body braced on top of hers, weight just barely registering, Jackson kissed her shoulders, one at a time. He worked his tongue, teeth and lips along the upper planes of her body until she was limp, clinging to him for support because there was no strength left in her.

Satisfied that there was no longer any question in her mind that he was hers and intended to remain so for all time, Jackson brought her to the final leg of their emotional journey.

There, amid the tangled pieces of their clothing, beside the Portacrib which swayed lightly in the breeze coming in through an open window, Jackson took her. Took her into his heart, into his life.

Into paradise.

"You're mine now, Mallory. Now and always."

"Yes. Yes." The final word was more of a gasp as the rhythm they created together took them to where they both wanted to be.

Together.

# Twelve

---

**D**awn nudged aside the night with rose-tipped fingers, widening its grasp as it slipped silently through the slits in the bedroom blinds until it covered everything it touched.

Rousing, Jackson opened his eyes. There was no feeling of disorientation enshrouding his brain the way there had been at times when he'd wake up in one of the numerous places his nomadic lifestyle took him to. He knew exactly where he was. Exactly where he wanted to be.

Exactly where he intended to be for the remainder of his life. Waking up in bed beside Mallory.

She was curled up next to him, one hand flung over his chest. His gut tightened just to look at her. When he thought of what he had come so close to losing, he could almost feel his blood running cold.

But he hadn't lost her. Last night had irrevocably proven that to him.

They'd made love all through the night, taking a respite

only to feed the baby. Joshua had been amazingly cooperative, Jackson mused.

Mallory murmured something in her sleep and turned to the side. Jackson slowly inched his way into a sitting position, taking care not to wake her.

Maybe there was something to what Mallory had said about Sally having a magic touch. It had certainly been the most peaceful night they'd spent since Joshua had come home from the hospital.

Peaceful. His mouth curved in a smile. Well, that was true as far as the baby went. As far as they went, it had been tumultuous. And fine. So very fine. His body hummed like an aftershock just remembering the way she'd felt in his arms.

If there had been any doubts in his mind about the wisdom of returning, about the wisdom of aligning his life with one woman, one place, it was gone now, burnt away in the heat of last night.

He'd never gotten around to hearing what she'd initially wanted to say, he realized now. But last night hadn't been a time for words. Only actions. Only feelings. And hers went as deep as his.

She loved him. He was certain of it.

With his world finally set right, he could afford to be generous. Jackson actually felt sorry for Steven, freezing his assets in the wilds of Alaska, but that wasn't his affair.

Or maybe, he amended, it was. Mallory would have never sought solace in another man's arms if he hadn't been such a coward.

If he hadn't run from what he knew in his heart was his destiny. If he hadn't been afraid of making a mistake. He'd couched his reasons in a lie, even to himself, saying he was afraid that she was taking away his life's forces and sucking him dry so that there was nothing left to put down on a page.

The problem was, running scared, he just hadn't thought to channel his consumption with her correctly. There was plenty to spill out onto a page. Being with Mallory aroused so many emotions within him, it made him want to write forever.

But that, he thought smiling, watching her sleep, would be an incredible waste of energy. A man had to feed his soul sometime. Loving Mallory most definitely did that.

She fed his soul, his imagination, everything.

He was through with lies, to himself and to her. He needed her. Both her and that little being in the other room who had so tenaciously wrapped himself around his life, just the way his tiny hand had wrapped around his outstretched finger.

God, he felt alive, renewed. Invigorated.

Ideas began multiplying in his head like rabbits in season, creating a mood. He had to get some of this down before he forgot it. Jackson thought of his computer, but that was on the desk in his room. He loathed the idea of leaving Mallory just yet, her body still warm with sleep and loving.

Maybe there was something in her nightstand he could use just to jot down a few buzzwords that would trigger him later.

Computers were a godsend, he thought, but there was still nothing like the feel of putting pen to paper. There was something very basic and fulfilling about it.

He glanced at Mallory, his heart swelling. Basic and fulfilling. Like making love to the one woman in the world who inflamed his senses and sent his creative juices flowing.

Silently sliding open the drawer in the nightstand on his side of the bed, Jackson looked in.

"Good girl," he murmured under his breath. Along with what looked like a manual of instructions for the digital alarm clock on the stand, was a pen and two pencils. That meant, he assumed, that there had to be something to write on as well.

Sliding the drawer farther open, Jackson began to rummage for a pad or a clean sheet of paper. He took out a handful of papers beneath the manual and quickly thumbed through them, looking for something he could use.

He stopped when he found it.

It wasn't a large piece of paper. Quite harmless looking, really. Just a birth certificate, nothing more. But it caused Jackson's heart to stop beating right in his chest when he read the words on the document. And then started it up again with a vengeance that throbbed in his temples and poured like stinging lava through his veins, incinerating everything it came in contact with.

There, in the place where it said Father, was his name. Jackson Cain.

He was a father. He was Joshua's father. Jackson was numb.

And then he was angry.

Shifting, Jackson looked at the sleeping woman beside him. The woman he would have risked betting his soul on. The woman he would have sworn couldn't utter a real lie if her life depended on it.

The first thing he'd asked her when he had seen her standing there in the real estate office was if the baby was his. And she had said no.

She had lied to him. And despite everything to the contrary, at bottom, he had believed her. Because Mallory wouldn't lie.

Harnessing the anger vibrating through him with steel bands, Jackson placed a hand on Mallory's shoulder and shook her. The next instant, he pulled his hand back, afraid that if he touched her again, he wouldn't be able to contain the pure rage he felt at this moment.

How could she have kept this from him?

Mallory woke up with a start, then rubbed her eyes. Had she dreamed the sudden, rude jerk on her shoulder? "What is it? Is it the baby?"

Jackson's voice was low, dangerous. "Yes, it's the baby."

Immediately alert, she began to rise. The odd tone in his voice only registered belatedly, as Jackson grasped her arm, pulling her back against the bed. She turned toward him, drawing the sheet up against herself, instinctively knowing something was wrong.

"What is it?"

"I should be asking you that." Jackson thrust the paper in his hand toward her. "What is this?"

Oh God, he'd found it. He'd found Joshua's birth certificate. Everything turned to dust inside of her.

Acting on instinct, defensive, Mallory pulled the document away from him. "How did you get that? You had no right to go through my things."

He couldn't believe that she had the audacity to be annoyed with him.

"No right?" He raised his voice. "No right? You're a hell of a one to talk about rights. You had no right to keep this from me." He heard himself shouting. With effort, he lowered his voice. Even a decibel lower, it sounded like a growl. "Why didn't you tell me?"

He had no right to be angry with her. He'd given up all rights by leaving. "I was protecting Joshua."

She made him sound like a creator that ate its young. "From what? An ogre?"

The hurt in his eyes was coated with fury. Leery, she wanted to pull away. But running wasn't going to solve anything. And it wouldn't help clear the air. It had been tainted long enough. If the matter was out in the open, she'd deal with it.

"No, from a charismatic man who would weave in and out of his life, leaving Joshua behind without any regard for his feelings."

And she still wasn't certain that he wasn't capable of just that. Nothing had been proven last night except that she still burned every time he was near her. But she already knew that.

For a moment, Jackson was silent. Just what sort of a monster had he led her to believe he was?

"You thought I'd do that to him?"

She pressed her lips together. "You did it to me and I thought I meant something to you."

He struggled to put his anger aside. To really place himself in her position. He was a writer, for God's sake. It was his job to look at things from perspectives other than his own. To look and understand.

But this was so close to home. It made it that much more difficult.

"You did," he said fiercely. His hand played upon her shoulder, a touch turning into a caress. "You do."

"But not as much as your work." She bit her lip. She would have chosen her time and place differently, but this was as good as any, she supposed, to finally have it out. "I didn't want to take you from it. I just wanted to borrow you once in a while. I would never have asked you to give it up," she insisted softly. "But you didn't understand that."

"No," he agreed. And they had both suffered for it. "I was too busy being afraid."

"Afraid? You?" She couldn't picture him ever being afraid of anything.

A smile curved his mouth as he nodded. The red rage of anger forgotten, he slipped his arm around her and brought her closer to him. "Yeah, me. Afraid of a magnificent woman who had me so tightly wound up around her finger, I couldn't breathe."

He made her sound manipulative, controlling. She shifted, looking at him accusingly. "I never did that to you."

He knew better. "Yes, you did. Without meaning to, you did. I couldn't think for wanting you, couldn't see my way into tomorrow without you. I was afraid that if I stayed, I wouldn't be me anymore. That wanting you would take away who and what I was."

She read between the lines. "So you're leaving. Just as I said."

How had she drawn that conclusion? "No, I'm staying. Just as I want." He moved her closer to him again, this time holding her firmly in place. He pressed a kiss to her temple. "I was right. There isn't a tomorrow without you." He tucked his arm around her under her breasts. "But I was wrong when I thought I couldn't write again if I stayed. I can. I have."

He thought of the novel that was so quickly taking shape. The process had never gone so smoothly for him before. "Maybe this is just an ego trip, but I think it's the best work I've ever done. Because I've never been happier."

She loved the thought of him being happy, but she was realistic, too. "Doesn't that take the edge off the brooding author?"

That's what he would have said once, but no more. "No, this way, I get rid of any dark emotions I might have by putting them down on the page. Purging myself. Mystery writers don't have to live like homicidal maniacs to write about them and I don't have to be constantly miserable to write about the underbelly of life." Right now, he was as far from miserable as a man could be.

Afraid to let herself believe too much, she felt her way around the topic slowly, like a blind man in a new place. "So then you're staying?"

"I'm staying." He nuzzled her, breathing in the sweet scent of her body. "Better tell Steven to get his manly shirts with the pins in them out of my side of the closet."

There was going to be endless teasing about this, she could just feel it. "There is no Steven."

"No?" He raised his brows. "What a surprise." Lowering his head, he kissed the swell of her breasts just above the sheet. "But there is going to be a Jackson. From here on in." He realized he was making assumptions for her. He didn't take kindly to being controlled, and neither did she. "If you'll have me."

"Have you what?" Mallory stared at him, more afraid to hope than ever. Because she wanted it too much. "What are you saying?"

He took her hand in his. "Mallory Flannigan, will you marry me?"

She wanted to, oh how she wanted to. But one of the reasons she had for not telling him was still intact. "Is it because of the baby?"

Jackson saw it as a package deal. Or a prize. Like winning the lottery. "He's part of it."

She studied his face, trying to discern the real reasons. "Just part?"

That leeriness was back in her voice. He hated it, because it was directed against him. "Yes, just part. I don't want to risk losing you again. When I thought you were living with another man, it ripped me apart. I put up with it because I thought I deserved it for walking out on you. I don't ever want to go through that kind of hell again."

He was serious. A smile began to build from the bottom of her toes. "What about your free spirit? Won't that be in jeopardy if you marry me?"

He had her, he thought. He could see it in her face. Jackson breathed a sigh of relief and told her what was in his heart.

"Free is just another term for rootless. I've done rootless. I want roots, Mallory. Real roots. Roots that twine my life with yours and Joshua's." He smiled. "Up until now, I'd say that Joshua represents my best work. I'd like to remain around him to see how he turns out." She hadn't answered him when he asked the first time. He tried again. "Will you marry me, Mallory?"

She pressed her lips together, this time stifling a sob. She'd wanted to hear that for so long. Ever since, she realized, she had first laid eyes on Jackson sauntering into the real estate office, looking for a place to temporarily call his own.

And now he was calling her heart his own.

"Yes. Oh, yes." Mallory slid back down against her pillow, an open invitation in her eyes. "So, what do we do now?"

He laid down beside her, gathering her to him. "Oh, I think something'll come to us."

Her eyes danced, her skin warming beside his. "Like making love?"

He pretended to mull it over. "Good idea. After all, we're already dressed for it."

And then he sealed her mouth with his, hoping to get in one more journey to paradise before their son decided to wake up and summon them.

\*   \*   \*   \*   \*

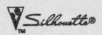

## MILLION DOLLAR SWEEPSTAKES

# BEGINNING IN APRIL
# FROM

**SILHOUETTE® Desire®**

*The Wedding Night*

Three passion-filled stories about what happens when the wedding ring goes on...and the lights go out!

**In April**—A kidnapped bride is returned to her husband in
FORGOTTEN VOWS by Modean Moon

**In May**—A marriage of convenience turns into so much more in
INSTANT HUSBAND by Judith McWilliams

**In June**—A once-reluctant groom discovers he's a father in
THE PRODIGAL GROOM by Karen Leabo

*THE WEDDING NIGHT:* The excitement began when they said, "I do."

STEP

INTO

THE

A collection of award-winning books
by award-winning authors!
From Harlequin and Silhouette.

Available this April

# TOGETHER ALWAYS

## by DALLAS SCHULZE

### Voted Best American Romance—
### *Reviewer's Choice Award*

Award-winning author Dallas Schulze brings you the romantic
tale of two people destined to be together. From the moment
he laid eyes on her, Trace Dushane knew he had but one
mission in life...to protect beautiful Lily. He promised to save
her from disaster, but could he save her from himself?

Dallas Schulze is "one of today's most exciting authors!"
—Barbara Bretton

Available this April wherever Harlequin books are sold.

WC-4

"Motherhood is full of love, laughter
and sweet surprises. Silhouette's collection
is every bit as much fun!"
—Bestselling author **Ann Major**

This May, treat yourself to...

# WANTED:

# MOTHER

Silhouette's annual tribute to motherhood takes a
new twist in '96 as three sexy single men prepare for
fatherhood—and saying "I Do!" This collection makes
the perfect gift, not just for moms but for all romance
fiction lovers! Written by these captivating authors:

## Annette Broadrick
## Ginna Gray
## Raye Morgan

"The Mother's Day anthology from Silhouette is the
highlight of any romance lover's spring!"
—Award-winning author **Dallas Schulze**

MD96

# As seen on TV!
## *Free Gift Offer*

With a Free Gift proof-of-purchase from any Silhouette® book,
you can receive a beautiful cubic zirconia pendant.

This gorgeous marquise-shaped stone is a genuine cubic
zirconia—accented by an 18" gold tone necklace.
**(Approximate retail value $19.95)**

## Send for yours today...
## compliments of ▼ *Silhouette*®
™

To receive your free gift, a cubic zirconia pendant, send us one original proof-of-
purchase, photocopies not accepted, from the back of any Silhouette Romance™,
Silhouette Desire®, Silhouette Special Edition®, Silhouette Intimate Moments®
or Silhouette Shadows™ title available in February, March or April at your favorite
retail outlet, together with the Free Gift Certificate, plus a check or money order for
$1.75 U.S./$2.25 CAN. (do not send cash) to cover postage and handling, payable
to Silhouette Free Gift Offer. We will send you the specified gift. Allow 6 to 8 weeks for
delivery. Offer good until April 30, 1996 or while quantities last. Offer valid in the U.S. and
Canada only.

## *Free Gift Certificate*

Name: _____

Address: _____

City: _____ State/Province: _____ Zip/Postal Code: _____

Mail this certificate, one proof-of-purchase and a check or money order for postage
and handling to: SILHOUETTE FREE GIFT OFFER 1996. In the U.S.: 3010 Walden
Avenue, P.O. Box 9057, Buffalo NY 14269-9057. In Canada: P.O. Box 622, Fort Erie,

---

## FREE GIFT OFFER
ONE PROOF-OF-PURCHASE

079-KBZ-R

To collect your fabulous FREE GIFT, a cubic zirconia pendant, you must include this
original proof-of-purchase for each gift with the properly completed Free Gift Certificate.

**079-KBZ-R**

# COMING NEXT MONTH

It's Silhouette Desire's 1000th birthday! Join us for a spectacular three-month celebration, starring your favorite authors and the hottest heroes of the decade!

## #991 SADDLE UP—Mary Lynn Baxter

One night with Bridget Martin had cost April's *Man of the Month*, single dad Jeremiah Davis, his bachelorhood! But would his new bride be the perfect mom for his little girl?

## #992 THE GROOM, I PRESUME?—Annette Broadrick

*Daughters of Texas*

Maribeth O'Brien was everything Chris Cochran wanted in a woman. So when she was left at the altar by her delinquent groom, Chris stepped in and said, "I do"!

## #993 FATHER OF THE BRAT—Elizabeth Bevarly

*From Here to Paternity*

Maddy Garrett had never liked arrogant Carver Venner. But now he needed her help—and Maddy couldn't resist his adorable daughter...or the sexy single dad!

## #994 A STRANGER IN TEXAS—Lass Small

One passionate encounter with a handsome stranger had left Jessica Channing one very pregnant woman. Now the mysterious man was back, determined to discover Jessica's secret!

## #995 FORGOTTEN VOWS—Modean Moon

*The Wedding Night*

Although Edward Carlton claimed his lovely bride had left him on their wedding night, Jennie didn't remember her husband. But she'd do anything to discover the truth about her past—and her marriage....

## #996 TWO WEDDINGS AND A BRIDE—Anne Eames

*Debut Author*

Brand-new bride Catherine Mason was furious when she caught her groom kissing her bridesmaid! So she went on her honeymoon with handsome Jake Alley—and hoped another wedding would soon be on the way....

# You're About to Become a

## *Privileged Woman*

Reap the rewards of fabulous free gifts and benefits with proofs-of-purchase from Silhouette and Harlequin books

# Pages & Privileges™

It's our way of thanking you for buying our books at your favorite retail stores.

✂

```
PROOF OF
PURCHASE          SD-PP115
Offer expires October 31,1996
```

**Harlequin and Silhouette—
the most privileged readers in the world!**

For more information about Harlequin and Silhouette's PAGES & PRIVILEGES program call the Pages & Privileges Benefits Desk: 1-503-794-2499

SD-PP115